The First Hard Times

D1495531

YEARLING BOOKS are designed especially to entertain and enlighten young people. Charles F. Reasoner, Professor Emeritus of Children's Literature and Reading, New York University, is consultant to this series.

For a complete listing of all Yearling titles, write to Dell Publishing Co., Inc., Promotion Department, P.O. Box 3000, Pine Brook, N.J. 07058.

The First
Hard Times

BY DORIS BUCHANAN SMITH

A YEARLING BOOK

Published by
Dell Publishing Co., Inc.
1 Dag Hammarskjold Plaza
New York, New York 10017

Yearling ® TM 913705, Dell Publishing Co., Inc.

ISBN: 0-440-42532-8

Reprinted by arrangement with The Viking Press

Printed in the United States of America

First Yearling Printing—May 1984

CW

For Willie,
who has known the adjustment
of a scrambled family

The First Hard Times

chapter 1

"Ancil, no!" Harvey's voice snatched at her from across the yard.

Arms poised in midair with a load of brush for the fire, Ancil turned. The way she stood, arms extended, looked as though she were presenting him with a gift of oleander clippings. What now? she thought. She was doing her best to cooperate.

"Ancil, uh, Ancil. Don't put those on the fire, uh," Harvey said. All the "uhs" were in place of the sugary words he used with her sisters. She had told him she wasn't his honey or darling or sweetheart. Her name was Ancil.

"Uh, Ancil," he said, striding across the yard toward

her, clippers in hand. "Those are poisonous."

"Poisonous!" She flung the clippings away from her and jumped back. Flames leaped to the clippings, all yellow and orange and blue.

Harvey rushed to the clippings, dragging them out of the fire with the tip of the clippers. "No, not poisonous to carry," he said. "Poisonous if you eat them or . . ."

"I wasn't going to eat them," Ancil snapped.

". . . if you burn them. The smoke is poisonous."

"You would have poisoned me," Zan said. "The smoke was coming right at me."

"I'm sorry, uh," Harvey said. "I didn't mean to bark at you, but . . ." He left his sentence unfinished as he picked up the scattered clippings. "Let's put these at the curb for tomorrow's trash pickup."

"What's going on?" Margaret asked, strolling across the yard, trailing the rake.

Lydia walked behind Margaret on the trail of the rake. "Yeah," Lyddy said. "What's going on?"

"It's nothing, sweethearts," Harvey said.

"Ancil was going to throw oleander clippings on the fire," Zan said.

"Ancil! Didn't you hear Daddy tell us they were poisonous?" Margaret asked.

"She never listens," Zan said.

"It's all right," Harvey said. "No harm done." He put a hand on Ancil's shoulder, and she hunched herself away from his touch.

I listen, Ancil thought. She listened more carefully than any of them knew. All this honey, darling, sweetheart, Daddy stuff. She stalked to the house, slammed the front door, and ignored her mother's call from the studio. She stomped up the stairs of the monster house and flopped onto the bed in her solitary room. Harvey probably followed her across the yard. Mother probably came to the door of the studio. The two of them probably arched eyebrows, shrugged shoulders, and said, "What's wrong with Ancil now?"

The air conditioner blotted out the intense Georgia heat, and its hum blotted the outside sounds. She could no longer hear the snap of the clippers or the scratch of the rake or the hollow thump of the out-of-balance wheelbarrow wheel.

How could they call him Daddy? Especially Margaret and Lyddy, who did have some real memory of their father. Ancil envied them that. All she had was the picture of him sitting in the rocking chair, holding her, her hair flaring scarlet from her baby head. Margaret and Lydia had the memories and Alexandra had his name. All she had was her waiting, the knowledge of her faithfulness.

The stairs creaked and she braced herself for the stern lecture or the soft soap, but no one came. Hands folded behind her head, she examined this dream of a room that had been hers for a month now. It was flooded with all her favorite colors, every shade of blue from cerulean to steel. And turquoise, like her eyes. A life-size stained-glass parrot flashed sunlit colors from the eastern window. There was even a rose trellis and roses that climbed up and peeked in her window. How she hated it!

How awful it had been to have to move to Hanover for the last month of school! Why hadn't they let her stay with Gran and Grandy and finish sixth grade in Juniper, where she'd always lived? And now that school was out, she had no cousins or friends to play with. And Zan was so pleased about having her own room that she hardly played with Ancil any more. They used to be sisters, two by two. Margaret and Lydia. Ancil and Zan. Now Margaret was more and more prissy every day and Lyddy was less and less so. And Zan, at almost eleven, was more and more like Margaret.

Eyes roving, Ancil spotted the olive shell on her dresser. Lloyd, her friend at school, had given her the thumb-size seashell. It reminded her that she did have one friend, but she wouldn't see him now that school was out. She sighed, but the thought of him made her smile. He had been so hateful to her at first, so infuriating, calling her "spaghetti head" because of her stringy red hair. How she would like to hear him say it now. She hopped up and plucked the olive shell from the dresser and turned it in her hand. At first glance it appeared to be only gray and brown, but if she really looked, she could see yellow and blue and green.

Thinking about Lloyd, large and shy and fierce all at once, she wondered where he lived. He had walked to the Rec Park for Shafer's birthday party, so he couldn't live very far away. Her brain clicked and she ran to Mother's bedroom for the phone book. Lloyd Albert. Albert. On the first page of the listings. There was only one, on Whitaker Street. She wondered if her name, Witherspoon, would be on the last page. No, it wouldn't. In Juniper, maybe, but not here. Here in Hanover the number would be in Harvey's name. Harvey Hutton. Owner of the weekly newspaper, the *Hanover Historian*. "Reporting history as it happens." All those H's. Ancil added some H's of her own and trotted down the stairs and opened the door to the studio without knocking.

"Mother, where is Whitaker Street?"

"Mmmmm," Mother said without looking up. Ancil grimaced. She'd blundered in again.

"I'm sorry, Mother. I forgot." They weren't supposed to go into the studio without knocking, and they weren't even supposed to knock unless it was an emergency. Harvey had them on the yard brigade partly to keep them out of Mother's way. This was the first week of vacation from school, and they hadn't yet adjusted to the habits of summer. For one thing, during school she didn't have to remember that Harvey was home on Thursdays. The paper went to press on Wednesday, and Thursday was his day off.

Mother finished a few brush strokes, then looked at Ancil's feet.

"I'm sorry," Ancil said again. She shrugged and grinned and looked at her feet. There was a family joke about what was and what wasn't an emergency. Years ago Mother had told them that if their feet were on fire, that was an emergency.

"Come here, sweetheart," Mother said. The word "sweetheart" sounded exactly right from *her* mouth. Ancil moved forward, and Mother caught her in a hug and nuzzled her neck with kisses. "I love you so much," Mother said. "So-o-o very much. You know that, don't you?"

"Yes'm," Ancil murmured, melting into the embrace. She loved the warm softness of her mother's skin and the smell of paint. "Where's Whitaker Street?" she asked again.

"It's just one block over. The street that runs right into the entrance of the Rec Park. Why?"

"That's where Lloyd lives," she said, feeling a little stupid not to know the name of a street a block away. But, then, she'd paid as little attention as possible to Hanover. "You know, the one who gave me the olive shell?"

"Yes. Well, that's great he lives so close. Perhaps you will have a summer friend, after all."

As Ancil nodded in response, a joyous cry went up from outside.

"They're here! They're here!" It was the grandparents arriving for a beach picnic.

Ancil and Mother rushed out of the studio. Gran and Grandy were crossing the yard, hugging as they came—hugging Margaret, hugging Lyddy, hugging Zan, hugging Harvey. This last made Ancil pause. How could they hug Harvey? It was their very own son Harvey had replaced. But her own need for them, her father's parents, hastened her step. Gran scooped her up, and Grandy set Zan down and hoisted Ancil up, still strong enough to boost her to his shoulders as she knew Daddy would if he were here. Zan was younger, but Ancil was smaller. Sometimes it had its advantages.

"Come see the kittens," Lydia said, grabbing hold of Gran's hand, pulling her along ahead of everyone else. Commenting on the yard and the heat, everyone tromped behind Lydia and Gran. They went inside, upstairs, to see Bridey, the white wedding cat, and the newborn kittens.

When Mother and Harvey married five weeks ago, Harvey had given each of the girls a wedding present. Harvey said they could choose, and Ancil had chosen extravagantly. In a beautiful color-coordinated gift shop called The Sea Garden there was a wonderful stained-glass parrot. Ancil had dreamed of it and never expected in her whole life to have it. When Harvey asked, that was what she'd named, and, incredibly, he'd bought it for her. He hung it at the east window in her room in the new-old house. Every morning the glass parrot said, "Good morning from Harvey," in green and blue and red and purple. The parrot, a macaw, was more beautiful than it had ever been in The Sea Garden shop. But the shining sunrise colors were a daily reproach for not liking Harvey.

Margaret's choice had been clothes, clothes, clothes to make just the right impression in the new school. And on Donnie Duggan, next door. Zan, also extravagant, had wanted and received one of the pouchy-faced dolls that came with name, birth certificate, and adoption papers. Zan collected dolls, and now that Zan had this particular stupid doll, she treated it as real and didn't need Ancil for a roommate.

Lydia's choice had been Bridey, a pregnant white cat from the Humane Society. Not for Lyddy a Persian or Siamese or Burmese or Himalayan or Manx, any of which Harvey would have bought her. Lyddy was fifteen and wanted to be a veterinarian. She worked part-time at the Humane Society and wouldn't have any cat except one from there. She wanted one that was an almost-grown female, because she herself was an almost-grown female. And she wanted the white one not only because it was her favorite but because white was for weddings, even though Mother's wasn't.

They crowded around the closet, the adults letting the children in front. Everyone oohed and ahhed over the kittens. There were four of them—an orange, a tabby, and two white ones, like Bridey.

After a quick look at the kittens, Margaret said, "Let's go to the beach now."

Lyddy was stooping over the cat box, holding the little orange kitten, her favorite. She'd already put in to keep it. "Yeah," Lyddy said. "Margaret thinks if you've seen one kitten you've seen them all."

"No," Zan said. "What Margaret saw was Donnie Duggan leaving for the beach."

"I want to get a tan," Margaret said.

Gran and Grandy circled them in hugs before they let

them out of the confines of the edge of the closet.

"Me, too," Harvey said, and he reached out for them as they started for the door, but he only caught Margaret and Zan. Lyddy was still in the closet, and Ancil side-shouldered past.

Everyone helped carry stuff to the car, then Ancil and Lyddy climbed into the back of the old station wagon with the stuff. They knew their places. Zan always leaped for the middle of the front seat to secure herself between Mother and Harvey. Gran and Grandy took up most of the back seat and Margaret had to be allowed the space beside them. As the oldest, she thought herself too sophisticated to ride in the back of station wagons. Lydia would never be too sophisticated for anything, and, Ancil decided, neither would she.

The beach was wonderful, as always. Even Harvey's presence couldn't spoil that. They spread the two beach blankets on the sand, and Ancil smeared her freckled self with sunscreen. She asked Lyddy to do her back so Harvey wouldn't offer.

The girls, all but Margaret, headed to the water and kicked high as they leaped each approaching wave. Last one to get wet above the knees was the winner. Margaret sauntered about, glancing up and down the beach. Ancil thought it amusing that out of eight miles of Golden Isle Beach Margaret thought Donnie Duggan would be on this exact spot.

As the tallest, Lyddy managed to leap the edges of waves

the longest. Zan next. It was embarrassing, Ancil thought, to have a little sister who was bigger. Besides that, Zan was such a high jumper.

Waist deep, Ancil let Lyddy and Zan go on ahead. She gave herself to the water, floating back and forth parallel to the beach, letting each head of foam push her shoreward. Margaret came in and passed Ancil to join Lyddy and Zan beyond the breakers. Zan was a fish and could handle any amount of water. Ancil couldn't swim and wouldn't risk going beyond the breakers without Mother. In close, now, still floating, she let her hands crab-walk through the sand. Every once in a while she felt the rise of a sand dollar just beneath the surface. She'd pick it up and pop it down inside her bathing suit so she wouldn't have to run in and out of the water. She remembered when she was younger, coming to the beach from Juniper forty miles away, she thought a sand dollar was worth a dollar and she gathered a hundred. She had felt so poor when she learned she wasn't rich.

Seeing the adults on the blankets, nibbling, made Ancil feel hungry. She crab-walked to the shallows until her entire body was scraping sand, then she stood up and ran to the blankets.

"I'm hungry," she announced, fishing the sand dollars from her bathing suit and tossing them onto the sand. Harvey, with a hand full of potato chips, poked one toward her mouth. Her mouth opened and received it before she could tell it not to. She chomped her teeth on the chip, crunching it vigorously. Her mouth liked the taste in spite of the fact that the chip came from Harvey's hand. Didn't that man ever quit? His pale skin was turning pink in the sun. She hoped he'd blister. "Give her time, give her time," she'd overheard Mother telling him when they were having a discussion about why Ancil was not adjusting. She wondered how the others could adjust. Especially Gran and Grandy. Never mind that Dad didn't have a chance to have his say. Sure. Time. About sixty-two years might be enough, she guessed.

"Let's get in the water before we eat," Mother said. She hopped up, grabbed Ancil's hand, and raced for the surf. Harvey, of course, was right behind them. And Gran and Grandy, too, though they walked instead of ran. They enjoyed the water as much as anyone else and had been coming to Golden Isle Beach off the coast of Hanover for years. They'd brought their children, including Ancil's father, Alexander. He'd raced across this very sand.

Mother held Ancil's hand firmly and swooped her up over the breakers as they went beyond. Zan paddled about like a baby whale, taking water into her mouth and spouting it. Zan spouted at Harvey and he ducked her. Soon they were playing, Zan using Harvey's underwater knees as a diving platform and plunging headlong into the waves. Ancil leaped every approaching wave, holding hands with Mother, riding the crest, dipping into the trough.

"Throw me," Zan said to Harvey as she stood poised on his knee. He put his hands at her waist and tossed her into the next wave. Mother looked at Harvey and Zan, smiling to see them having such fun together. Sixty-two years, Ancil thought, floating up to the next peak, Mother's hand going up, helping Ancil mount the wave. Harvey threw Zan higher each turn. Zan shrieked through the air, disappeared beneath the dusky water, then porpoised back to Harvey.

"I'll bet Ancil can go even higher," Harvey said. Ancil's "No" and Mother's "No" were lost as the breakers churned behind them. Harvey's hands were at Ancil's waist. He was tossing her up, not high like Zan. It was just a small toss, but there she was heading for a wave and no hand to hold hers.

Eyes wide open, she saw the murky yellow-green of the water as it enfolded her. She rolled head over tail and tail over head, grabbing at water but finding no handhold. She didn't know which way was up or which was down. There was one solid scream inside her, but her mouth did not open to let water in. Suddenly she was sputtering and hands were grabbing for her. Margaret, Lydia, Harvey, Mother, Gran, Grandy were a twelve-armed octopus. Like an infant, she knew her mother's hands. She leaped for them and clung, arms coiled around Mother's neck, legs wrapped around her waist. She buried her face in a nest of wet hair—her mother's, her own—sputtering, gasping, sobbing.

"She can't swim," Mother said stonily to Harvey.

"Oh, my God, Laura. She can't swim? I didn't know. I didn't mean . . ."

Mother waded toward shore, and waves swished at Ancil's waist. The water lapped at Ancil's bottom, snatching at the seat of her bathing suit, trying to get her back. Harvey hovered, walking along beside them, apologizing to Ancil, apologizing to Mother.

"It's okay. She's all right, thank goodness," Gran said.

"It wasn't your fault," Margaret said.

"Yeah," said Zan. "She never tells anybody she can't swim."

Waves licked at Ancil's feet, then she was at last free of the seizing sea.

"Let me take her," Grandy said, but neither Ancil nor Mother would relinquish the grip they had on each other. Harvey was still murmuring beside them. Ancil raised her head from Mother's shoulder and looked at Harvey with her turquoise eyes that matched some seas but not this one. This sea was the color of cat's eyes.

"You tried to drown me," she said.

chapter 2

They wanted her out of the way. Ancil knew it. Harvey wanted to drown her and make it permanent. Mother simply wanted it temporarily. The household would be more settled with her gone. She knew that, too. They weren't fooling her any. But after they returned from the beach, Gran and Grandy offered to take her home with them. She couldn't turn down a chance to go to Juniper.

Really, it was Lydia's turn to be Grandy and Gran's "special." All through the years they'd taken turns by age, oldest to youngest, and Margaret had been the "special" last. But Lyddy was reluctant to give up her work at the Humane

Society even for a weekend in Juniper. Weekends were the busiest times. What a fine coincidence for them all that she was next in age, Ancil thought. A totally convenient way to be rid of her. But staying in Juniper was what she had wanted all along.

She sat in the middle of the back seat, arms resting on the top of the front seat. Her feet were on the drive shaft, and her knees came almost to her chin.

"Water on my side, water on my side," she droned absently. Her mind was whirling, twirling, trying to think of how she could parlay one weekend in Juniper to forever.

She didn't even realize she was singing until Grandy said, "No fair. You're in the middle. You have water on both sides!"

Ponds and drainage ditches lined the roadside. Years ago, to alleviate the boredom of the long straight south Georgia road, one of them had started the "Water on my side" chant. It was sung in a four-beat measure, three beats on the same note with the last note two intervals below. Grandy joined in, a third below her, harmonizing. Gran tuned in a third above, and they sounded like a barbershop quartet minus one.

Ancil laughed. She was going home to Juniper, forty miles away from Harvey, Hanover, and any beach. She would sleep in her own father's bed. She stared off through the rows of planted pines that lined the other side of the drainage ditches. The pine trees looked as though they were walking on stilts. Everything was so straight. The road, the trees, the rows of pines. Even the shadows were straight.

At the house she marched right upstairs to secure her things in Dad's room. The pale blue walls, the navy blue quilted spread and drapes that were faded to purple, surrounded her with comfort. And there on the dresser was the picture, a copy of the one she had, the last picture they had of him, him holding her as a baby. She lingered over it for a moment, startled to see Margaret in his face. Why had she never noticed how much Margaret looked like him? The dark hair, the same facial features. Zan and Lydia were blond like Mother. Ancil herself had red hair that popped up from nowhere.

She glanced for a moment at the elaborate model ship Dad had built when he was sixteen, then she ran back downstairs.

In spite of having had sandwiches for lunch in Hanover, they also had sandwiches for supper, and they all made their own. There was the same routine here at Gran and Grandy's that there was at home. Some days were do-it-yourself days in the kitchen, and other days they took turns.

"You won't malnutrish from one day of sandwiches," Gran would say if anyone commented. Ancil couldn't remember when anyone had.

As she lifted a circle of bologna to construct her sandwich, Ancil suddenly noticed something different in the kitchen. "Oh," she said in surprise. "What's, uh, it doing in here?" A sculpted head of her father at age sixteen was beside the sink. Gran had done one of him and one of Uncle Ran when they were boys. Ancil was surprised to see Margaret again. She'd never noticed that Margaret looked like Daddy. Was it because Margaret was almost sixteen? She looked at Gran and Grandy for resemblance to Dad and Margaret. Except for the dark hair, she found none.

"Just wait till I tell you what I'm doing," Gran said.

"Yes," Grandy said. "Just wait till she puts straws up your nose."

"Straws up my nose?" Ancil said, wondering what that had to do with the statue of Dad's head on the kitchen counter. "What's he doing in here?" The heads were usually on pedestals in the entry hall by the stairway, and she hadn't noticed before that Dad's was missing.

"Well-l-l." Gran and Grandy were working together making a salad, Gran slicing lettuce and tomatoes, Grandy chopping peppers, cheese, mushrooms, and onions. "I'm making life masks," Gran said. Ancil and her grandparents finished their supper preparations at the same time and put sandwich and salad on the table and sat down to eat.

"I'm working on a special project that I don't want to tell about yet, but I'm making masks of everyone in the family, and since—well . . ." She shrugged. "I couldn't do Alex except to copy the sculpture. So I made a mold of it. That's what it's doing in here. I have to wash the Vaseline off."

"Where's the mask?" Ancil asked.

"In the studio. I want to do yours tomorrow. I've already done Ran's family."

"Jennifer, too?" Jennifer was her same-age cousin. They were best friends and had been in class together at school before Ancil moved to Hanover.

"Everyone but your grandfather," Gran said. "Perhaps you can help me persuade him."

Grandy shook his head. "Nobody's going to put straws up my nose," he said. He glanced at the head of Alex, perched beside the kitchen sink. "If you're good enough to get that likeness, you can do a likeness of me the same way, then make a mask the same way. She didn't put straws up *your* nose, did she, Alex?"

Ancil laughed, delighted at this inclusion of Daddy as though he were really here.

"Or your own, yet, either, have you?" Grandy said to Gran.

"Well, I would if you'd help me," she said.

"Nobody's putting straws up my nose, and I'm not putting straws up anybody's nose," he said.

"I've been trying to get someone to help me do my own mask," Gran said. "Perhaps you'll help me, Ancil."

Ancil nodded. She didn't even know what they were talking about—straws up the nose! But she would help. One of her favorite things to do in the world was help Gran in the ceramic studio. She even knew a lot about glazes and firing the kiln.

After supper she was the one who washed the Vaseline from the sculpted head of her father. Using very warm, soapy water and a clean dishcloth, she washed her father's face and hair and behind his ears.

"The Vaseline's just on the face," Gran said.

"Don't get soap in his eyes," Grandy said.

She couldn't help getting soap in his eyes since Vaseline was in his eyes, but she apologized for it. She held his head back and thought about him bathing her when she was a baby. He was good with the children, everyone said. Good with Margaret, Lydia, and herself. He didn't even know Zan was born. Probably didn't even know Mother had been pregnant with Zan.

In bed that night, in Daddy's room, she thought of Zan and how they weren't friends any more. Since Harvey. Since moving to Hanover and having separate rooms. Here, at least, she was used to sleeping in a room by herself, without Zan. All their lives, until five weeks ago, they had shared a room. They'd fussed sometimes, but not much. Ancil had enjoyed sharing a room. Going to sleep at night, they'd talk. Then, if Zan fell asleep first, she listened with pleasure to the sound of Zan breathing. Such a comfortable, companionable sound, someone breathing in the same room.

But Zan had leaped eagerly at the idea of having her own room in Hanover. Ancil had had the idea that they could still share a bedroom and use the other room for a playroom. But Zan, new little mother with her life-size dumpling-faced doll, wanted her own room, was delighted to have her own room. Zan didn't miss sharing with Ancil at all.

Now Ancil's eyes roved about this room. Dad had had his own room. And Uncle Ran had had the room next door. But since it was a big house and there had been only the two boys, they'd had an upstairs playroom too. The rigging of the model ship made black lines against the black space. Dad had built the ship about the time Gran did the sculptures, when he was sixteen and Uncle Ran thirteen. Grandy built model ships, too, and sold them for a lot of money.

Ancil's eyes traced the dark rigging, glad that the ship was still there on the dresser, that Dad's room was here, waiting. The room and herself. That was all that was waiting. The house down the street where he'd lived with his wife and children was lived in by someone else. There was no room waiting for him in Hanover, where his wife and children now lived. There was no wife waiting for him. Laura Witherspoon was now Laura Hutton. And three of the beautiful daughters, even the one who looked like him, called another man Daddy. The thought pierced her.

MIA, she thought. Missing In Action in a war that was over before Zan was even born. A war in a place called Vietnam had stolen their father. He had parachuted from his disabled plane and was alive when he landed, and that was the last news they had of him. He could be alive, she thought. He could. Sometimes on the news there were reports that MIA men had been seen over there, in prisons.

What would it be like, she wondered, to be in prison in a strange country all these years? She dismissed the thought. Some nights she let her imagination put herself in his place, to experience everything he might have experienced, even torture. He might have been through more than a person could bear, she knew. And tonight, after having washed his face, it was more than she could bear.

Still, she could not be like the rest of them, like Mother, who said, "It is less painful to think he is dead." Yes. Ancil agreed that was less painful. Less painful for them to act as though they knew something definite. Less painful for Daddy, too, if he was dead. But she wanted the pain. The pain meant hope. The pain meant that he might be alive and one day, one day, come home. She would be waiting.

chapter 3

In the morning she saw the masks. Daddy at sixteen, Uncle Ran at thirty-two. The younger brother had become the older.

The clay Gran had used was Georgia red clay, which gave the faces the complexion of the traditional flowerpot. "They look like Indians," Ancil said. "You could make a totem pole."

Gran looked at her in surprise. "Can you keep a secret? A very-very secret?" Ancil nodded. "It's a surprise, and I'm only telling you because, without even knowing it, you guessed."

"What?" Ancil didn't know what she had guessed.

"Totem poles. I *am* making totem poles. Family totem poles. I'll make the rest of your family's masks when we take you home Sunday. But suppose we mold our masks this morning. Yours and mine. Let me do you first, then you'll have some idea of how to do mine."

Gran cut a plastic straw in half and handed the two pieces to Ancil. "Here, practice breathing through them. Go on, put them in your nostrils," Gran said when Ancil hesitated.

A little reluctantly Ancil slid the straws into her nostrils. Feeling like an idiot, she snorted laughter, and the straws fell out.

"Laugh, laugh," Gran said. "Get it out of your system because you're going to have your face covered with plaster, and you'll have to be still."

Ancil replaced the straws, shut her mouth, and breathed. Air traveled through the tunnels of the straws. All the while explaining the procedure, Gran dipped into a jar of petroleum jelly and greased Ancil's face, even her eyelids and into the edge of the hairline. Unsure about the whole thing, Ancil lay on a sheet on the floor of the studio. Jennifer had done it, and Uncle Ran and Aunt Cath, and even little Randy, who was only six. But Grandy had not. She tried to form a protest inside her head, but before she had worked it out, Gran was applying plaster and murmuring for Ancil to keep very still.

"Relax and breathe easily," Gran said.

The plaster was cool against her cheeks, but it would get

warm, Gran had said. Ancil concentrated on her breathing. In, out, in, out. The plaster pressed against her face. What was the word for being afraid of closed-in places? Hypochondria? No. Phobia? Hydrophobia? No, something about being shut in a closet. Closet, closet, claustrophobia. Yes. Claustrophobia. The plaster began to warm up.

"It won't get too warm to bear," Gran reassured her. Still, Ancil was beginning to think she had claustrophobia. "Just a minute now. Almost done." Gran had finished adding plaster and was waiting for the set. Ancil felt the breath coming through the straws to her nose, but she still felt she was smothering. Smothering. Drowning.

"Mmm-mm," she said, thrashing her way up through cat-eyed water. As she came up, Gran struggled with her, pulling the mask free with a suctioned slurp. Air, air, saved from drowning. Into Gran's arms.

"Oh, my Ancil. Sweetheart. It's all right." Gran held her and set the plaster mask on a table. "I'm sorry. I didn't think. You must have felt like you were drowning."

Ancil nodded, clinging to Gran for a moment, though not as fiercely or as long as she'd clung to Mother after coming out of the real water yesterday. Gran's acknowledgment released her. She could see. Here she was on dry land, the dry, dusty land of the ceramic studio with the high ceilings and all the space.

"It's okay," she said, taking in and releasing huge gulps of air. "I'm okay. But it was scary for a minute. I think I have claustrophobia."

"I should have let you do mine first," Gran said. "So you could see what it would be like."

The terror was over. It was not the same as yesterday, having the ocean water lap at her while Mother waded out of the water. She craned around Gran to see the mask. She looked into her inverted face, where nose and lips and chin were dents instead of bumps.

By the time she'd washed her face and hairline, Gran had greased her own face and mixed the plaster and settled down on the sheet. "Just dab carefully at first," Gran said. "Make sure it gets into the corners of my eyes and mouth and around the edges of my nose." It was quite fun, actually, dribbling plaster onto Gran's face, thickening the layers, feeling the plaster warm up as it set. When Gran's "Mmm-mm" signaled that time was up, they both eased the mask off, and there was Gran. Ancil laughed at the sight of her, greasy and rimmed with white.

"Gran," Ancil said, "you're plastered!"

The plaster had to dry, and it would be tomorrow before they could make the actual masks. So, after lunch, Ancil decided to go to the pool. Uncle Ran and his family were on vacation, but her other friends would probably be at the pool.

As Ancil started out the door, Gran said, "Don't forget your money." Money? The knowledge startled her. Mother had always bought a family pass for the season. Ancil had never had to pay to get in the pool. But they didn't live in Juniper any more.

On the sidewalk she walked off toward Uncle Ran's, toward her former house, toward the street that led off to the recreation center. Her eyes and feet knew every line, every crack. She and Jennifer had played marathon hopscotch up and down this sidewalk.

Every house was familiar to her. There were the huge old frame houses with columns and porches and balconies, like her grandparents'. And there were smaller ones, of frame or brick, that had been built in between, as some of the old families had sold off parts of their large yards. The mixture of sizes and types of houses suited her much more than the new areas where houses and yards were so much alike. Suddenly she stopped and looked up and down the street. This totally comfortable, familiar street was, she realized with a start, very much like Princess Avenue, the uncomfortable, unfamiliar street on which she lived in Hanover. Horrible Hanover. Hateful Hanover. Harvey's Hanover.

Even the very houses, her grandparents' and Harvey's, were similar. And Gran and Mom both had studios. Ancil stomped her foot in protest and quit her noticing. She didn't like the thought of Hanover and Harvey intruding into her Juniper head. At the house where she used to live, one of the small ones, strangers were now living. If Mother hadn't married Harvey, if she still lived here, Ancil wouldn't have to carry money to the pool.

She started across the wide expanse of grass that was a shortcut to the pool. This grass was as familiar as the sidewalk. They'd played stoop tag, shadow tag, Red Rover, and all sorts of chasing games here. In the distance were fenced fields, where Little Leaguers were playing baseball. The crack of bat against ball, the *rat-a-tat* chanting calls caused her to grimace. Hanover again. At school in Hanover you were liked according to how well you played baseball. Which meant she wasn't liked at all.

One of Margaret's boyfriends was tending the entrance to the pool. "Hey, Witherspoon," he said. "Where've you been? Haven't seen you around lately."

"We moved," she said, looking at him in surprise.

"Moved? Where to?" he asked.

She handed him the dollar, and he handed her a small wire basket for her clothes. Didn't he know they had moved? Margaret would be furious, Ancil thought. "Hanover," she said.

"Oh, Hanover. The beach. Aren't you the lucky one," he said. "I'd like to live in Hanover."

Did everyone in the world but her like baseball and beaches? she wondered. She forgot that until yesterday she'd liked beaches quite a bit herself. "I don't call it lucky," she said. "I'd rather live in Juniper."

"But the ocean," he said.

"You can have it. I almost drowned in it yesterday."

"Did you really? How? Don't you know how to swim?" He sounded full of concern, as though swimmers didn't sometimes drown, she thought. She shrugged and stepped toward the dressing room. "We have swimming lessons starting next week," he said. "You ought to come."

Swimming lessons, ugh! she thought. Margaret would be interested. Margaret had always liked swimming lessons, though not for her love of swimming or water but because of the boys who sometimes taught them. Ancil laughed to herself. And now this last one didn't even know Margaret had moved.

The dressing room was empty and rang with echoes of herself. Her friends would be out by the pool. They would be happy to see her. She changed quickly, poked her clothes into the basket, plunked the basket onto the counter in front of What's-his-name, and walked through the footbath to the apron of the pool.

The sun was blinding off the turquoise water. The damp, warm, chlorine air filled her nose and lungs. Such a summer smell, she thought. Voices and splashing filled her ears. Shielding her eyes from the glare, she strolled around the pool, looking about for her friends.

"Here comes Ancil With-her-spoon," a young voice called.

She squinted, smiled, then waved. It was the little brother of her classmate Jill. Former classmate, she reminded herself. "Hey," she said to him.

"Hay's for horses and you're a cow," he said, giggling.

"Cows eat hay, too," she said, wondering if she was ever that silly. To give him satisfaction, she made a face.

"Well. Ape, then. You're an ape."

Around the pool she saw and spoke to several people she knew, but where were her special sixth-grade friends? The greetings were casual. Hey. Hey. How are you? Fine. Me, too. Jennifer was on vacation, but they couldn't all be on vacation. Where were Jill and Karen and Tammy?

When she passed him again, she asked Jill's little brother. "Where's Jill?"

"In Washington," he said. "You know. Why didn't you go?"

Washington? She said the word with an upturned end, as though it were a question, but it was not. It was a realization. Washington! The sixth-grade trip. She'd forgotten. In one month she'd forgotten the Juniper sixth-grade graduation trip. "Hah!" she said to Jill's brother, as though it were his fault she wasn't with them, his fault she hadn't even graduated. Here in Juniper she would have been starting junior high in the fall. In Hanover they had what they called Middle School, and sixth grade was the first year of it. She repeated her walk around the pool, squinting, looking for any particular friend. Washington. She'd moved, been away for only five weeks, and the only people who knew it were in Washington.

She stepped into the shallow end of the pool and let herself slide underwater. She pressed her feet to the side of the pool and pushed off. Underwater she could swim. Underwater she was a fish. With her eyes open, she moved her arms and finned past a forest of legs. When she reached the other side she popped to the surface and caught her breath. Then she hoisted herself to the side of the pool and walked, dripping, to get her clothes.

"Hey, you didn't even get your dollar's worth," What's-his-name said.

She snatched her clothes from the basket. "Hay's for horses and you're a jackass," she said. Somehow it had turned into his fault, too, that they'd moved, that he hadn't even missed them.

"Don't forget swimming lessons," he said.

"Why didn't you tell me Jennifer was in Washington?" she said, still dripping when she walked into the studio, where drips didn't matter.

Gran's fingers were guiding clay into a large cylinder shape on the twirling potter's wheel. "But you knew that," she said, without looking up.

"I forgot," Ancil said, sorry there wasn't someone to accuse. "Nobody's even here."

Gran slowed the wheel with her feet, ran the cutting wire beneath the cylinder and lifted it off the wheel head. "You're here and I'm here, and that's the most important thing."

"I'm the first one to miss the trip," Ancil said. Margaret and Lydia had gone in turn. "I don't see why we had to move," she said. "We could at least have stayed until the end of school."

Gran centered another lump of clay and resumed kicking the wheel. "We've had this conversation at least sixteen times," she said. "I really don't see any point in having it again, do you?" Gran's fingers pressed into the clay and brought it out to a diameter of about ten inches. She checked the width with calipers before she began bringing it up. "I love you and Grandy loves you. Your mother loves you and Harvey loves you. You are a much-loved girl. But you are going to live with your family, and that's all there is to that." Gran raised the cylinder to a twelve-inch height and again slowed the wheel. These cylinders, joined together, were going to form the core of the totem pole.

"But you're family." Ancil made one more stab. "You and Grandy are family."

Gran slid off the bench and gave Ancil an arm hug, holding her wet clay hands out, away from them. "Ah, Redbug. You know what I mean."

"I just don't understand how one new person in the family can have so much power over the others. Five of us lived in Juniper and only one lived in Hanover. Why didn't Harvey move to Juniper? It doesn't seem fair." They'd had this conversation sixteen times, too. Harvey's business wasn't portable. Mother's was. But who cared, who cared, who cared? Everyone cared, apparently, except her.

"How would you like to empty the kiln for me?" Gran asked. Ancil knew that if she said anything else on the subject she'd only be talking to herself. And she'd had the conversation with herself a hundred and sixteen times.

On Saturday morning Ancil and Gran each pressed clay into her own mask mold. In the afternoon she went with Grandy to the building site of a house he'd designed and where he was supervising the construction. The house was in the country, by a pond, and, except for the bathrooms, it had glass walls.

"Oh, Grandy, I love it," she squealed. "I want a house like this."

"Curtains or drapes would spoil the effect," he said. "You couldn't live in town with a house like this. And you're a town girl, aren't you?"

She shrugged. She'd always lived in town, but she didn't know if she was a town girl.

"You couldn't get back and forth to the pool from here," he said.

"I could swim in the pond," she said. "And if I wanted a pool I could build one, couldn't I?"

He laughed and put a hand on her shoulder. "You're planning to be mighty fancy, aren't you?"

She responded to his laugh and his touch by leaning against him as they returned to the car. Excitement leaped inside her, but she contained it. An idea had rolled around in her head. Pool. Swimming. Swimming lessons. Everyone wanted her to learn how to swim. She wanted to stay in Juniper, and the recreation center in Juniper was about to start swimming lessons. How perfectly it would work out! Without saying where the lessons were going to be, she mentioned swimming lessons to Grandy, then to Gran. They were both enthusiastic.

On Sunday they returned early to Hanover. Gran had mask molds to make. Ancil felt like a professional assistant, having already experienced straws in her nose.

"Do we have to?" Margaret asked, while Zan giggled about the idea of straws up her nose.

"Everyone has to," Gran said.

"Even me," Grandy said. "In fact, I'll be first. You can get all that giggling out of your system while you watch me." He poked Zan in the belly with his index finger. Had his reluctance just been teasing, Ancil wondered, or was he making a special effort to set an example for Margaret?

"Now don't crack jokes or he'll crack his plaster," Gran said when Grandy was all greasy-faced and Ancil began to apply plaster. She and Gran took turns. Grandy, Lydia, Zan. When Margaret saw how easy it was, she, too, was agreeable.

"I think I'd like to learn how to swim," Ancil said casually while Gran had Margaret under plaster. "You know. Take swimming lessons."

Mother and Harvey looked at one another and exchanged expressions of delight.

"I think that can be arranged," Harvey said, as Gran lifted the plaster mask mold from Margaret's face. Everyone admired the inverted Margaret, and Mother, already greased, lay down for her turn.

"They're starting lessons in Juniper tomorrow," Ancil said as she put the first blob of plaster on Mother's face. Bridey strolled in and sniffed at the plaster.

"Oh, Bridey, do you want your mask made too?" Lydia asked, scooping the cat into her arms.

"I don't think she'd sit still for straws in her nose," Gran said.

"Smart cat," Grandy said. "By the way, how are the kittens?"

"Oh, they're darling," Lydia said. "They've grown so much. Come see."

As Ancil thickened the plaster on Mother's face, Lydia, Grandy, Zan, and Margaret left the studio. Plaster hand in the air, Ancil gazed after them without realizing it.

"Run along," Gran said. "I'll finish."

"Oh, no," Ancil said, returning her attention to the masking. But when she'd finished her part, she washed her hands, left Mother on the floor, and ran to see the kittens.

chapter 4

Monday morning. First day of swimming lessons in Juniper. And here was Ancil, walking east on Princess Avenue on her way to swimming lessons. In Hanover.

Princess Avenue. She lived her life on Princess Avenue. Home. School. Home. School. Even Harvey's newspaper office was on Princess Avenue, though she had been there only once, under family pressure. The school, which fronted on Queen Street, backed up to Princess. At the end of Princess Avenue, she crossed Sidney Lanier Boulevard onto the Rec Park grounds. This town was crazy with streets named for kings and queens, princes, princesses, and poets, Ancil thought.

She'd been this far only once before. Shafer's birthday party. The thought was no comfort, though Lloyd had helped her triumph.

"Hey, Ancil. Spaghetti-head!" someone called as she crossed the grass. She looked up. It could only be Lloyd, and it was. No one else in Hanover bothered to speak to her. "Going to swimming lessons?" he asked.

Where else? she thought, wishing the tight roll of towel with her bathing suit inside were invisible. Of all the people she should have wanted to see, Lloyd was the one. It was almost as though her thought had summoned him. But she didn't want anyone, even Lloyd, to see her on her way to beginners' swimming class. Little Fish, they called it. Cripes!

"Me, too," he said, assuming her destination, even though she hadn't replied. Lloyd carried a bathing suit and towel hanging loose from one hand.

"Basic Rescue?" she asked, assuming his destination. While the Little Fish were learning in the shallow end of the pool, a group of advanced swimmers would be practicing life-saving methods in the deep end. Ancil thought the combination was ironic.

"Basic Rescue? Oh, no." He laughed his warm bubbly laugh. "I'm going to be a Little Fish. Don't you think that's funny? Me, a little fish?"

More like a baby whale, she thought, but saying it would be either mean or humorous. She certainly wasn't feeling humorous. Why was he so delighted to be going to a swimming class called Little Fish?

"You got your bathing suit on under?" he asked, looking at her rolled-up towel.

"Nah. It's in here." She joggled the rolled towel for emphasis.

"Hey, neat. How did you learn to do that?"

"My, uh, Harvey did it for me."

"Harvey? Is that your brother?"

"We just have girls in my family," she said. "Except for, uh, Harvey."

"Oh, yeah, that's right. I remember you told me. And none of you play baseball, right?"

"Right." Their names were checked off a list at the gate, and they were allowed through to the dressing rooms. Ancil looked around at the aqua-painted concrete walls and the row of hinged doors to the dressing room stalls. Just like Juniper. And she felt just as at home as she had at the Juniper pool the other day, which was not at all.

As she started out of the dressing room, she saw Marcia from school. Marcia saw her, too. They looked at each other, not quite certain whether or not to speak.

"Hey," said Ancil quietly, half hoping Marcia wouldn't hear.

Marcia heard. "Hey, back," Marcia said. "You coming to Basic Rescue?"

Ancil shook her head.

"Little Fish?" someone else said. Ancil looked and there was a whole delegation from sixth grade at Hanover Middle School. Shafer, Bobby, Kirby, none of whom had been friendly with her during her month at their school. She didn't know who'd said, "Little Fish?" She didn't comment but walked toward the shallow end of the pool.

"Hey, Lloyd, you coming to Basic Rescue?" she heard someone say. It was probably Kirby, but she didn't look. Kirby was a friend of Lloyd's but not of hers. Lloyd was the only friend she had in this dumb town. How come she saw none of her schoolmates in Juniper, where she cared, and a legion of them here in Hanover, where she didn't?

"Little Fish," she heard Lloyd say in response to Kirby. Lloyd sounded so proud of himself, as though Little Fish were the top class.

"Little Fish?" That was Marcia's voice. "You mean *she's* just in Little Fish?" Marcia's words turned into giggles. Ancil felt herself go as red as her hair.

"Both of us," Lloyd said.

"Well, uh, you have to start somewhere," said Kirby.

Their words pushed her on to the shallow end. As she approached, a high school boy was organizing the class. "I want all my little fish to sit at the edge of the pool with their feet in the water," he said. Several children plopped to the side of the pool and began kicking their feet in the water. Two or three held back. They all looked about five or six years old.

All my little fish indeed, Ancil thought. She whirled and almost bumped into Lloyd, who was right behind her.

"Hey, Ancil, where're you going?" he said.

She didn't answer; she just kept going. She asked for her basket, scooped her clothes out of it, and walked away. The scene was a rerun of the other day in Juniper, except this time she hadn't even gotten wet.

"Who is it?" Mother called as Ancil came in.

"It's me," she answered.

"Me, who?" Mother said, coming out of her studio, brush in hand. Who did she think it was? Ancil wondered. Margaret was working for the summer at Harvey's newspaper office, Lyddy was at the Humane Society, and Zan was at day camp. "Oh, Ancil. What are you doing back?" Mother had on jeans and the white intern jacket she used as a painting coat.

"I decided not to take swimming lessons," Ancil said.

"But, Ancil, sweetheart, you wanted to. It was your idea."

How could she tell Mother that her idea was to stay in Juniper? "Everyone there is five or six years old," she said, which, except for Lloyd, was true and also part of her reason. "I'm not about to be called a little fish!"

"Ancil, sweetheart." Mother hugged her with the paintbrush held aloft. Rerun of the arms hug, too, Ancil thought, except it was Mother instead of Gran. "You do need to learn to swim. It would mean so much to me if you would."

Ancil steeled herself against all persuasion. "I didn't mean to disturb you," she said. "Go on back to work."

"Yes, yes, okay," Mother said. "I have to get this jacket design finished. We can talk about it later." She ducked back into the studio and closed the door.

Mother did various types of free-lance artwork, from

paintings, to book jackets and illustrations for children's books, to advertising. That's how Mother had met Harvey, doing ads for a client who advertised in the *Hanover Historian*.

Ancil relished the almost empty house. She knew she wasn't going to bump into some tense situation with Harvey on the next stair or in the upstairs hall. Even her room comforted her. The morning sun was still pouring through the window. Shards of color from the parrot flung themselves across the room. At the same moment that delight thrust upward within her, remembering the source of the parrot squelched it. She *had* wanted the parrot, but she'd asked for it only to be—well, saucy. In her family such gifts as stereos, personal TVs, and expensive parrots were not given. Those things came when you were old enough to work and save and buy them for yourself, as Margaret and Lydia were beginning to do. Ancil had never dreamed Harvey would give her something so expensive.

On impulse, she took her swimming towel, pushed the desk chair over to the window, stood on it, and covered the parrot. There. The fragments of color disappeared from the room. She hopped down from the chair, shoved it back beneath the desk, and crouched at the window, elbows against the sill, chin in hands. The man next door, Mr. Duggan, was on his upper deck with his telescope. Mr. Duggan was an astronomer of some sort, Margaret said. Because of the Duggans' son, Donnie, Margaret knew all about the Duggans. Margaret had suddenly become interested in the stars. What could he be looking at in the daylight? Ancil wondered.

The doorbell sounded below, a melodious *bing-bong*.

"Ancil, would you get that, please?" Mother's voice followed the bell tone up the stairs. Ancil shoved herself away from the window and, still in her bathing suit, clattered down the stairs. She flung the door open, ready to call Mother to the door or to tell the caller that Margaret, Lydia, Zan, or Harvey was not here. But it was Lloyd, in his regular clothes, hair wet from the pool, soggy towel and swimsuit under his arm.

"Hey," he said softly, ducking his head shyly. She was so surprised she just stared. "Why did you leave?" he asked. Heat pushed in with his voice. She seldom noticed heat except in contrast to the air conditioning.

"How did you know where I live?" she responded.

"Shafer showed me," he said.

"Shafer! How did he know?"

"Who is it?" Mother called out.

"He lives on this street. Right down there." Lloyd pointed down Princess Avenue.

Shafer on her street? Shafer the snob prince on Princess Avenue? She should have known. Bad-luck town, bad-luck street. When she didn't answer, Mother came to the door of the studio.

"Oh," Ancil said. "I'm sorry. This is Lloyd Albert—you know, the one who . . ."

"Yes, I know," Mother said. "Lloyd, who gave you the

olive shell." Mother transferred the slender paintbrush from her right hand to her left. Then she swiped the empty hand across her once-white painting smock and extended her hand to Lloyd. "Hello, Lloyd. I'm Ancil's mother, Mrs. Hutton. I'm so happy to meet you."

Lloyd grinned and bobbed his head from side to side. "Me, too. Glad to meet you, Mrs. Hutton."

Ancil opened her mouth and closed it again, grabbing her lip with her teeth. Hutton. Mrs. Hutton. Her mother, who had always been Mrs. Witherspoon, was now, really and truly, Mrs. Hutton. And there was nothing Ancil could do about it. She wanted to flee, but a combination of pain and politeness held her there, listening to Mother and Lloyd make conversation.

"Why, Ancil, I'm surprised," Mother said after a few sentences exchanged with Lloyd. "I would have thought you'd enjoy swimming class with Lloyd there."

"I'm not about to make a fool of myself learning how to swim in a baby swim class," she snapped.

"I'd think you'd make more of a fool of yourself if you don't learn," Lloyd said. There was innocence, not sarcasm, in his tone.

"Not if nobody knows that I don't know how to swim," she said quickly. Just as quickly Harvey, who hadn't known, sprang to mind. She looked at Mother as Mother's eyes darted toward her for the barest part of a second.

"Why don't you invite Lloyd to stay for lunch," Mother said, changing the subject. Ancil knew she and Mother were thinking the same thing—that Ancil had almost made a drowned fool of herself because of not knowing how to swim.

"Oh, no, ma'am, I couldn't," Lloyd said, shaking his head vigorously. The invitation seemed to fill him with embarrassment, and his embarrassment saved Ancil from the memory of the drowning fool. She stepped onto the porch to save him, in turn. Mother said a last glad-to-have-met-you and disappeared into the studio.

"Is your mother a painter?" Lloyd asked. "My mother works at the shrimp plant, and she wears a white smock that gets all messy, too. Smelly, too," he said, wrinkling his nose.

Ancil explained what Mother did.

"Come sit down," she added, moving toward the corner of the porch that spread out into a hexagon shape. "You can stay for a few minutes, can't you?" Sections of lattice arched between the columns on the porch, forming ovals and circles like old-fashioned picture frames. A rectangle of this same type of lattice climbed up the house in back, to Ancil's window. In the broad corner of the porch were wicker chairs and a basket swing. Ancil sat in one of the chairs. The swing had been Harvey's wedding present to Mother; she had always wanted such a swing.

Lloyd spotted the swing and gestured toward it. "Can I sit in it?" he asked in a high, soft voice. Ancil felt a surge of tenderness toward this large boy with the gentle voice. She hadn't noticed he had such a gentle voice. It hadn't been gentle when she had first heard it. He'd been snorting, "Spaghetti-head!" at her.

He set the wet wad of bathing suit and towel on the porch floor next to the railing. Then he backed into the swing, letting it catch him behind the knees before he gave his weight to it. When he picked up his feet, the single chain of the swing revolved as well as swayed, like a slowly spiraling pendulum. Lloyd rhythmically touched his toes to the porch floor to keep himself facing her. A grin as broad as a quarter moon shone from his face. "This is as much fun as swimming," he said. Pleased by his pleasure, she returned his grin.

"I learned how to swim today," he said, his voice as distant as though he were still at the pool. "In just one day I learned how to swim." He and the swing ebbed and flowed several times before he spoke again. "I'm going to learn to swim so well that Mama won't be afraid to take me to the beach."

"Oh?" she questioned, wondering if he, too, had almost drowned. "Why is she afraid to take you to the beach?"

He sat up, planting his feet flat against the floor, giving up the sway of the swing. "Mama is afraid for me to do anything," he said.

"Well, I guess she's not afraid for you to take swimming lessons," Ancil said.

"Oh, yes." He jumped up and plucked his towel and swimsuit from the floor. "I just told her I was going to, that's all."

And I'll tell Mother and Harvey I'm not going to, Ancil thought.

"In fact, I'd better go home. I was supposed to call her the minute I got home. She'll think I drowned." He shrugged and ducked his head in that half-shy way he had. "I just wanted to find out what happened, that's all. Are you coming back tomorrow?"

She shook her head. "No. But come by after. Will you?"

"If I can," he said, and he waved good-bye. The back of his shirt collar was dark from where his damp hair had dripped. The porch floor was dark where his towel and swimsuit had been. As he walked away, Ancil stared absently at the spot.

chapter 5

At the dinner table Harvey expounded on water safety. He was not pleased that Ancil had quit swimming lessons before they even began. But he knew, and she knew, his authority reached only so far.

"If you get caught in a tumble of waves," he said, "you sometimes don't know up from down."

Tell me, Ancil thought, forking broccoli hollandaise into her mouth. Margaret had cooked. She was even getting good at it.

"What you should do, Ancil, uh, is simply float. Try to relax and float, and you'll bob to the surface," Harvey continued. "Then you swim or let the surf push you ashore."

With Mother, Ancil could say whatever she thought or felt. Mother said that feelings were neither right nor wrong— they just were. But Ancil wasn't comfortable enough with Harvey to say what she thought. She usually kept her mouth shut. But with him talking about oceans and water, her mind quickly put her back to sailing through the air after he'd tossed her.

"I might need that advice if a wave ever catches me," she said, words spurting out in spite of her attempt to contain them. "Or if someone throws me in."

"Yes," Harvey said with no hesitation. "People do stupid things sometimes, like throwing someone into the water without finding out if the person likes being thrown into the water. And innocent people sometimes get caught in the middle, and they just have to handle it."

"I'm handling it," Ancil said sharply.

"The kittens almost have their eyes open," Lyddy said.

"Growing up doesn't make you perfect," Harvey went on, ignoring Lydia's attempt to change the subject. "Grown- ups do stupid things, too."

"Yeah," Margaret said. "Like the time Mother reached out for Zan to keep her from falling and wound up knocking her down harder. Remember?"

Mother groaned. "Don't remind me," she said.

"Margaret thinks she's so grown up," Zan said. "That's why she's so cooperative about household chores, like run- ning to the store for bread or milk."

"Shut up, you," Margaret said.

"There's a certain bag boy named Donnie," Zan continued.

"Mother, I'm going to kill her," Margaret said.

"He and his father have a telescope, and astronomy is Margaret's new favorite hobby."

Margaret jumped up from the table and started around toward Zan, but Mother caught her by the wrist.

"That's quite enough, Zan," Mother said. Margaret's eyes were narrowed to slits.

"Well, golleeee," Zan said. "If I had a boyfriend I'd be proud of it."

"Mother-r-r!" Margaret said.

Ancil thought Harvey had been effectively cut off. But the next morning she found herself plodding down Princess Avenue toward the Rec Park. It was Mother who'd insisted on the swimming lessons, but Ancil knew the order came from Harvey. She flapped her bathing suit and towel loose from Harvey's tight roll. Mother wasn't much of an insister except for necessary things, such as keeping the kitchen clean enough not to be a health hazard.

Ancil stared at her feet, at the sidewalk. Left foot, right foot, left foot, right foot. Her feet were familiar in the red sneakers, but she did not know this sidewalk. She'd followed it for a month, the last month of school, but she'd paid no attention to it. She had paid no attention to this sidewalk in particular or to Hanover in general.

As she crossed the grass of the park to the pool, she saw

Marcia, Shafer, Kirby, and Bobby standing around the gate. She wished there were some other way into the pool area. She didn't know whether or not to speak. She certainly didn't want to speak. She decided she would if they did. They didn't speak, and Ancil felt her face go red with embarrassment.

"Too bad she can't swim as fast as she can run," Shafer said as she passed between them.

"She can't run all that fast," Marcia said.

I can run faster than you, Ancil thought, but she forced herself not to turn around and respond. All they did every time they opened their mouths was prove how rotten they were. They'd been hateful to her from the first day at recess when they discovered she couldn't play ball.

Behind her, she heard the voices calling out to Lloyd. She held her hand out, and the girl behind the counter handed her a basket.

"Hey, Ancil," Lloyd called out, but she kept her back to him, too, and went into the aqua dressing room. When she'd first started at Hanover Middle School, they'd all been hateful to her, even Lloyd. They'd been hateful to him, too, in fact, until he'd smashed that homer at Shafer's birthday party. Now they thought he was okay. What kind of way was that to judge people, she wondered, by whether they could play ball or not, or swim or not? How many of them could make life masks or use a potter's wheel or fire a kiln? She could run backwards faster than Marcia could run frontwards. The word "backwards" triggered something in her head, and she suddenly saw Marcia's name back-wards. Aicram. Yeah, she thought to herself. I like that. Aicram!

Lloyd was waiting for her when she came out of the dressing room. "Hey. I'm glad you came back," he said, tilting his head to one side and hunching his shoulders.

"They made me," she said.

"Are you mad?"

"I'm not happy."

"Are you like my uncle?" They strolled toward the shal-low end of the pool and sat along the edge with the other little fish.

"Why in the world would I be like your uncle?" she asked.

Lloyd grinned. "He says he's very even-tempered. He just stays mad all the time."

Ancil looked at him. Apparently he thought that was funny.

From where he stood in the pool, the instructor said, "Okay, everybody into the pool to practice your kicks." At least he hadn't called them little fish. Ancil slid into the pool. Lloyd waded out chest-deep and started swimming. He must have already known how to swim a little, she thought. Well, she did, too. Underwater. Along the edge of the pool little fish gripped the side and splashed up a commotion. One little boy had refused to get in the pool. The instructor playfully dribbled water over his own and the boy's head, trying to coax him into the water. Ancil wished she could grab the child by the hand and lead the escape.

Lips pressed grimly together, she took hold of the side of the pool. When she kicked, her toes cracked the bottom of the pool. As she said, "Ouch," and reached to hold them, her face dipped into the water. She came up sputtering and coughing. If she grabbed the boy and ran, she wouldn't even know where to go. She had spent so much time hating Hanover that she hadn't paid attention enough to know any hidey-hole places.

"I'm sorry," the wonder-boy instructor said, coming over to her. "I forgot you weren't here yesterday." He showed her how to place her hands, one on the top edge of the pool, the other below the water, flat against the side of the pool. With the lower hand she was to brace herself, and the pressure of that hand would raise her legs. She was surprised to find that it worked. Her feet broke the surface of the water with wonderful splashes.

"You don't really have to splash that much," he said. "I encourage the little ones to do it because it's fun and it helps them get over being afraid." He explained that a proper kick barely broke the surface. Still, she continued splashing mightily. It was fun.

"You'll be out there with Lloyd in no time," he said. She stopped for a moment and looked at Lloyd, swimming as though he had always known how. She ducked beneath the water, eyes open, and watched the wavery line of kick-kick-kicking feet.

"I'm going to hate it," she announced to Lloyd as they toweled themselves at the edge of the pool.

"I'm going to love it," he said.

"I'll never learn," she said.

"Sure you will."

"Easy for you to say." She picked up her basket. "You're good at everything."

"Me? I'm not good at anything," he said, but she was already on her way into the dressing room.

"What am I good at? Name one thing," he said when they had dressed. His brown hair stuck to his head in clumps. Hers hung dripping down her back.

"Swimming," she said. "What other little fish can swim across the pool on the second day of lessons? And baseball. I'm the one who's not good at anything."

"Multiplication," he said quickly. The two of them were usually the last ones standing when they had multiplication bees at school. "And you have the prettiest eyes of anybody in the whole wide world. Like the color of the water in the Caribbean Sea."

Tenderness whooshed through her, like yesterday when she had noticed his gentle voice and enjoyed his pleasure in the basket swing on the porch. The sun warmed her suddenly, not in anger and humiliation as with Marcia, but in an easy glow, like the warmth of setting plaster. "But that's not anything I can *do*," she said. "Can you see me walking up to Marcia and saying twelve times fourteen is a hundred sixty-eight?"

"You mean you know past the twelve tables?"

"You just add twenty-four to a hundred forty-four," she said.

As Ancil and Lloyd passed through the gate, Marcia appeared, dressed, and dripping. "Race you," Marcia said.

"Hey, yeah," Lloyd said.

"Cram it, Aicram," Ancil said, and she walked off toward Princess Avenue.

chapter 6

Ancil walked briskly across the grass of the Rec Park. Children were on the playground, and swing chains clanked. Lloyd was in step behind her, but he didn't speak until they had crossed over to Princess Avenue.

"What's this Aicram business?" he asked, looking back toward the park. "And why wouldn't you race her?"

"Marcia, Aicram. Dyoll. Licna," she said, pointing at Lloyd, then at herself.

He scrunched his face in puzzlement, then said, "Oh, I get it. Backwards. It's our names backwards!"

She grinned at his quickness.

"But why wouldn't you race her? That's another thing you do well. Run. You could beat her running backwards. You run fast as the wind."

She smiled at his thought matching hers, running backwards. The only time he'd seen her run was at Shafer's birthday party when they'd given her a base on balls. He'd been up to bat next and hit a homer. She hadn't known it was going to be a homer, so she hadn't known she would have all the time in the world to get around the bases. She had run like the wind. And they'd all been amazed.

"Why didn't you ever hit the ball until Shafer's party?" she countered. They'd been even more amazed at Lloyd's homer. At school he had been the strike-out king, swinging widely at the first three pitches, whereas she never swung at all.

He ducked his head shyly. "I didn't want to," he said.

"That's why I didn't race," she said. "I didn't want to."

"But you could show 'em!"

She watched the sidewalk as she walked, watching for lines and cracks, trying to learn it and let it become familiar. If Harvey had his way, she'd be walking this way every day for at least two weeks. "Why didn't you show them?" she asked. "I mean before Shafer's party? You could have shown them. And why did you decide to show them then?"

He ducked his head again. "Because I didn't want to. Because you were on base." He gave her two answers for her three questions. "I didn't want to leave you stuck on base."

"Really?" A grin popped to her face. She hadn't known his hitting the homer had anything to do with her.

"I live right over there," he said. "On the next street." Yes, Ancil thought. Mother had said Whitaker Street was one street over. "In fact, there's my cat. Here, kitty-kitty." He started across the street toward a large striped cat. The cat turned and ran away. From the middle of the street Lloyd looked back at Ancil. "She's not really my cat," he said. "She's a stray, I think. Mama and I put out scraps and she sneaks up and eats the scraps, but she won't let me get near her."

"We have new kittens at our house," Ancil said. "They're just about to open their eyes. Why don't you come see them?"

"Do you think I could?" he asked.

"Sure. Why not?"

"Your mother wouldn't mind?"

"Of course not. Why would she?"

He bobbed his head, considering, thinking, deciding. "Okay, I think I will. I'll have to call Mama first, though. Okay?" At the corner Lloyd turned left.

"Where're you going?" Ancil asked.

"To call Mama."

"You can use our phone," she said.

"Can I? Yeah, well. Why don't I call from my house and you come with me, then you'll know where I live." She followed him down a side street where she had never set foot before. On Whitaker, Lloyd's house was second from the corner, one of the smaller houses, smaller than their house in Juniper and with no shrubbery. She stood on the porch and he went in.

"Come on," he said. "Come on in."

She felt awkward, going into the house when his mother wasn't home. She stood just inside the doorway while he disappeared into another room. She heard the whir of the dial and heard him tell his mother where he was going. There was silence, then Lloyd's voice again.

"I'm not calling to ask permission. I'm calling just to let you know where I'm going," he said. "I think I should be able to go somewhere for an hour without asking."

Ancil's eyes had been focused on the doorway through which Lloyd had gone. Looking around seemed intrusive, prying. But at the private turn of the conversation she moved her eyes around the room as though that would block her ears. His words startled her for a moment, his telling his mother instead of asking. Then she thought of all the places she went without asking. She'd just run out the door saying, "I'm going to Jennifer's." Or Gran's. In Juniper, anyway, not here in Hanover. She hadn't wanted to go anywhere in Hanover.

For the first time she saw the room. Sofa. Large television set. Two chairs. Against one wall, dominating the room, leaned a huge round slice from a tree. She could see the lines of the growth rings. There must be hundreds. The slice was as high as her head. When Lloyd re-entered the room, she asked about it.

"It's a tree from the yard," he said, walking to it and running his hand across the surface. "Three hundred sixty-two years old. Kirby helped me count the rings." He traced a few rings with his fingers. The tree slice was higher than his shoulder, Ancil noted, and he was tall for twelve. "We're going to have a table made out of it."

Outside, he showed her where the tree had been. "Mama and I nearly cried when they took it down," he said.

"Why did they cut it down?" she asked, unable to understand why anyone would take down such a magnificent tree.

"Lightning. It was struck by lightning. It was dead. The landlord was afraid it might fall on the house," Lloyd said.

They walked back toward Princess Avenue, and Ancil looked at the various-size live oaks with a new appreciation. "Funny," Lloyd said. "I never really paid any attention to that tree until they started to take it down."

His remark surprised her, especially since she'd been thinking about how she hadn't paid attention to Hanover. "There are a lot of things I haven't paid attention to," she confessed. "For instance, I've never been down that street before. I don't really know much about Hanover. I don't even know my way around."

He looked at her in surprise. "Me, either," he said. He pointed to the back of the school they were passing. "Would you believe I just recently found out that the back of the school was just two blocks from my house? Mama always takes me and picks me up from the front, on Queen Street, and that way it's four blocks."

"My whole life is on Princess Avenue," she said.

"I'm beginning to learn my way around," he said. "Walking, that is. I know my way everywhere in the car."

Ancil winced. She didn't even know her way around in the car, except that King Street became the highway that went to Juniper.

"Mama has always taken me everywhere. When I came over yesterday, it was the first time I ever walked on Princess Avenue."

They paused at the curb of the last cross street before Harvey's house. Ancil saw Mr. Duggan drive up and park in front of his house. She didn't know what kind of work he did as an astronomer, but he seemed to be around day and night.

"Mama's afraid something will happen to me," Lloyd said. "Not just that I'll drown. But that I'll get hit by a car or be kidnapped."

"Or a tree will fall on your head."

"Yeah." Lloyd laughed, seeming to take special pleasure in her remark.

Mr. Duggan alighted from his car and came around to the sidewalk.

"Mr. Duggan!" Lloyd said, rushing ahead on the sidewalk. "Mr. Duggan! What are you doing here?"

"Well, hello, Lloyd. I live here. Is that a good enough reason?"

"You live here right next to Ancil?" he asked, then turned to Ancil, "You didn't tell me you lived next door to Mr. Duggan."

She was going to make some remark, such as telling him she didn't go around making announcements about her neighbors, but Lloyd and Mr. Duggan were already involved in an animated conversation. Lloyd proudly told about being a little fish. Ancil wanted to crawl through one of the cracks in the sidewalk.

"Come over some night and look through the telescope," Mr. Duggan said to Lloyd. "You, too," he said to Ancil. "Why don't I ever see you? I see your sister all the time."

Ancil shrugged. She could tell him why he saw her sister all the time, and it wasn't because of a love of astronomy. Well, she'd leave Duggans and astronomy to Margaret.

"In fact, come around now and take a look at Venus."

"I didn't know you could see stars in the daytime," Lloyd said.

"Venus is a planet," Ancil said.

"It's often visible through a telescope in daylight," Mr. Duggan said. "Venus is the brightest planet. It's surrounded by clouds that reflect the light."

The next thing Ancil knew, Lloyd was following Mr. Duggan. "I have to go home," she said. "I have to let Mother know I'm home."

"We'll wait for you," Lloyd said.

"Come around to the back deck," Mr. Duggan said.

"No, I, uh, have stuff to do," she said quickly.

"I'll come see the kittens in a few minutes," Lloyd said. "Is that okay?"

She nodded and crossed her yard to the house. "I'm home," she called out to her mother. Mother called, "Okay," from the studio, and Ancil climbed the stairs to her room and looked out the window toward the Duggans' backyard. Lloyd and Mr. Duggan were already on the high deck. Mr. Duggan's mouth and hands were moving as he explained something to Lloyd. Why hadn't she gone with them? Had she stayed away just because it was Margaret's territory?

She saw Lloyd tilt his head and lean toward the eyepiece. What were these uneasy feelings? she wondered. Was it because Lloyd and Mr. Duggan knew each other? Was it because Lloyd's going over there indicated that Mr. Duggan was more important to him than she was? Yes. She nodded to herself in acknowledgment. He was her only friend, after all.

She plunked on the bed and put her hands behind her head. She seemed to be surrounded by Pied Piper people, and she was the only one not following. Harvey. Mr. Duggan. She looked at the picture of Daddy on the dresser. Even without him, all her life until three months ago had been so perfect. Mother had dated occasionally, but there was never anyone special. Even Harvey was okay at first, humorous and kind of nice. Then Mother announced she was going to marry Harvey. How could anyone take Daddy's place?

The doorbell rang and she didn't move. It rang again and Mother called out to her. Even though she knew it was probably Lloyd, she didn't answer Mother or the doorbell. Mother's footsteps sounded. The door from the studio opened, then the front door.

"Ancil," Mother called.

"Yes'm," she said. She struggled up from the bed and repeated her "Yes'm" over the upstairs railing.

"Lloyd is here."

Ancil looked down onto Mother and Lloyd standing in the entry. "Come on up," she said to Lloyd.

Lloyd looked at Ancil's mother for permission. Mother smiled and waved a hand to indicate yes, go on up. As Lloyd came up the stairs, Mother gave Ancil a look and returned to the studio.

"You should have come over," he said, and he began a monologue on Venus's atmosphere and the clouds that hide the surface. Just as he was telling her that Venus could be both an evening and a morning star, she interrupted.

"Want to see the kittens?"

"Yeah, sure. That's what I came for." He followed her into Lydia's room, still talking about Venus. "You should have seen it, Ancil. It appears to wax and wane, just like the moon." But the sight of the kittens stopped his Venus words. "Awww," he said, and he stooped to the box and held out a hand. Bridey sniffed at his hand. "Does she mind?"

"No. She's a sweet, friendly cat," Ancil said. "She loves everyone." She reached down for the orange kitten. "You can hold one. It's all right."

He took the striped kitten and crooned as he cradled it. "This one will look like Kitty-kitty when it grows up."

"Maybe you could have it when it's old enough."

"Could I? I wonder if I could?" he said softly in his wonder voice.

"I don't think Lyddy has that one promised yet," Ancil said. "I can ask her."

"I wonder if Mama will let me."

Ancil scooped up the other two kittens so they would have their share of human attention.

"I've never had a cat before. Or a dog. Or anything. Just me and Mama."

"That's how we used to be," Ancil said. "Just us and Mother. Before she married Harvey."

"Do you remember the day Bobby snatched my olive shell and I ran out of class?" Lloyd asked.

She remembered. Lloyd and Bobby had had a shouting match right there in the classroom, and when Mrs. Parker took the shell, Lloyd had shouted at her and run from the room. A few days later he'd given it to Ancil. She knew it was an important gift.

"Mr. Duggan's the one who got it from Mrs. Parker and gave it back to me," Lloyd said.

Ah, she thought, her mouth open slightly and her head nodding. That's why he had so eagerly followed Mr. Duggan. "What did he have to do with it?" she asked.

"He works for the schools. Some sort of problem solver or something. He has a son. And a stepdaughter."

"Yeah, Lydia's age. Long black hair." She made no comment about the son and Margaret.

"Look!" he said. "The kitten's eyes are opening."

She looked at the kittens in her arms and saw slits of blue shining eyes. "These, too. See? Oh-h-h," she said, then laughed. "Have you ever noticed that everyone says oh-h-h or aw-w-w when they see baby animals? But they're so cute. In another week these little ones will be playing with one another."

"Really?"

"Yes, really. Don't you know anything about kittens?"

"I've never had one. I told you it's just been me and Mama. Except the times she married." He looked at her. "Is Mr. Hutton your first stepfather?"

"How many do you think? Sixteen?" The question startled her.

"I've had two," he said. "Three fathers, counting my real one."

The announcement silenced her. The idea of a string of Harveys was appalling.

"I almost had another one, but I had such a fit Mama didn't marry him." Lloyd stroked the kitten and murmured in its ear. "Now I wish I'd been nicer." He kept rubbing the kitten, making soft sounds to it. "Me and Mama have had a lot of hard times."

Ancil stared at the kittens in her lap. The orange one, the two white ones who looked like Bridey. The idea of a succession of stepfathers whirled in her head. The past in Juniper, all bright and shiny blue, was growing dimmer in the distance. After a long time of not saying anything, just petting and crooning to the kittens, she said, "These are my first hard times."

chapter 7

After swimming lessons on Wednesday Lloyd came home with Ancil for lunch. She called out to Mother that they were home and led the way into the kitchen.

"White bread, wheat bread, rye bread," she said, naming things as she hauled them out of refrigerator and cabinets. "Peanut butter, jelly, mustard, mayonnaise, ham, bologna, salami, cheese. Lettuce, tomato, onion, pickles. Or we can mix up some tuna or make a fried egg sandwich. You name it."

"Can you really do all that?" he said, his voice going high in that cute way she liked so much.

"Well, of course," she said. Did he think she was dumb?

"Mama fixes every bite I put in my mouth," he said.

"Well, I'm not your mama," she said, gesturing at the things she'd spread out. "This is a do-it-yourself kitchen. Fix whatever you want."

He stood first on one foot, then the other, hands behind his back. "Can I have a ham sandwich?" he asked.

"Sure," she said.

"And a salami?"

"Sure."

"And a peanut butter and jelly?"

Three? she thought. But quickly she said, "Sure. Help yourself."

Ancil started with wheat bread, mustard, and mayonnaise and began to build her salami sandwich. She noticed him watching, copying her moves. Had he never made a sandwich before? she wondered, hardly believing it.

"This is fun," he said when he'd made one sandwich thick with bread, meat, cheese, lettuce, tomato, and pickles. Like hers. Except for a change of meat he made another just like it. Then he made the less complicated peanut butter and jelly. Ancil poured their milk and put it and napkins on the table.

"Are you all doing all right in there?" Mother said, calling from the studio.

"Sure," Ancil said.

"I'm just learning how to do things," Lloyd said, looking at his sandwiches with admiration. "Mama has always done everything for me. She's treated me like a prince. You know, the day of Shafer's birthday party? I walked to the Rec Park. That was the first time I ever went anywhere by myself."

Ancil bit into her sandwich to keep from having to respond. "Mmmmm," she said with her lips closed. Mother and Gran and Grandy had always encouraged Ancil and her sisters to do things by themselves. She busied herself with chewing to keep from staring at him. She could scarcely believe what he had just said. He sounded almost like a four-year-old. A little fish.

"Have you ever been to town?" she asked, thinking about her own ignorances.

"Sure. All the time, with Mama."

"I mean have you ever walked to town?"

He shook his head.

"Me, neither," she said. "Why don't we walk to town after lunch?"

He looked startled, glanced off in the direction of town and then in the direction of the studio. "Will she let you?"

"Of course she will. It's only six blocks. Closer than the Rec Park." Not having gone before had been her own decision, not Mother's.

"I'll call Mama."

She showed him where the phone was and heard him start talking. From what he'd told her about his mother, she imagined the questions and concern on the other end of the conversation.

"She says I can go for an hour," Lloyd said.

When they'd finished lunch and put everything away, Ancil called out to Mother. "We're going to town."

Mother responded with a surprised-sounding, "Oh?" then quickly said, "Okay. Have a good time."

From right in front of the house Ancil could see where the river was. To the west, as they walked down Princess Avenue, she saw where the city stopped, as though the river were the end of the world.

"Let's go to the river first," she said, and they walked right past Grand Square at the center of town.

"Hey, look, here's the newspaper office," Lloyd said as they walked in front of the *Hanover Historian* building. Ancil gave no indication that she had any connection with it.

"That's where Mama works," Lloyd said, pointing downriver toward one of the shrimp plants.

"Mmmm," Ancil said in acknowledgment.

She looked up- and downriver at the docks and the glistening water. Gulls alternately soared and floated, bobbing, on the water. Pelicans stood on pilings, looking like statues of pelicans. At night shrimp boats lined the docks, but now they were out at sea. Across the river were acres of green marshland and an uninhabited inland island. The salt smell of brackish water filled her nostrils.

Involuntarily she said, "Ahhh."

Lloyd grinned and added his own "Ahhh." "Have you ever noticed," he said, laughing, "how everyone who smells the sea air always says 'Ahhh'?"

Back at Grand Square they walked around the court-house, which was the centerpiece of Hanover. The square was actually a four-square-block area. The broad avenues of King and Queen streets were interrupted by the square. Traffic flowed around on the bordering streets, which on the north and south sides were Prince and Princess avenues. The grass was like a golf course green, and the huge live oaks were bordered by azaleas. Palms added the semi-tropical touch of south Georgia.

"I've been in the courthouse," Lloyd said. "When Mama goes to get her car tag." They walked along the walkway that circled the courthouse, examining the building.

Ancil had been in it once, two months ago. Harvey had dragged her along on the grand tour of Hanover. She had been a reluctant draggee and had not paid much attention.

"I guess we'd better not go in unless we have a reason," Lloyd said. Ancil agreed. At each doorway, though, they scampered up and down the steps, then began walking faster and faster around the circle until they were running. One thing Lloyd did not do well was run, and Ancil quickly left him behind. Streaking along like the wind, thinking how easily she could outrun Marcia, she almost ran into a man coming the other way.

"Oops," he said, catching her by the elbows and side-stepping her.

"Oops," she also said, following it with an apology. Her embarrassment made her giggle. She found Lloyd huffing and puffing, waiting on one of the sets of stairs. She plunged onto the step beside him, puffing a bit herself.

"I almost ran into someone," she said, still laughing with embarrassment.

He laughed, too.

"It's not funny," she said.

"You laughed first," he said, and in a moment they were both laughing, just from the giddy freeness of being there.

"I'm burning up," he said.

"My nostrils are on fire," she said.

"Your freckles are popping out," he said.

She looked at herself, her red arms dotted by the redder freckles. They did pop out by the minute in the summer sun.

"I like them," he said. "And your eyes. How many do you have, anyway?"

"Freckles? Fourteen million," she said. "And two eyes."

He took hold of her hand and began to count the freckles. She looked at their hands, his large pale one and her thin red spotted one. It was a fine thing having her hand held. Something inside her went *bloop*, and she suddenly thought of Margaret and Donnie Duggan.

Wednesday was Ancil's night to fix dinner. Usually she made hamburgers because they were pretty easy. Zan also fixed hamburgers. And if they cooked on Sunday evening, it was hot dogs or hamburgers. No one complained, because complaining meant having to fix dinner an extra night.

Exuberant from her afternoon with Lloyd, she decided

to really cook. She'd never used the cookbook, though Mother said it was easy. All you had to do was be able to read and follow directions. Mother or Harvey would instruct, or even help, in exchange for having equal help on their nights. Potato peeling, or something. Ancil was getting good at peeling potatoes without leaving half the potato in the skin as she used to. But no hamburgers tonight. Or potatoes.

She wandered into the kitchen and pulled the cookbook off the shelf and began to browse. No sooner had she settled down than she heard the back door open and there was Harvey coming in. She frowned into the cookbook in a show of concentration.

"Something special for tonight?" he asked, stomping his feet on the doormat.

"Mmmmm," she said, not looking up. What was he doing home? Wednesday was press day, and sometimes he wasn't even home for dinner.

"Early press," he said, clapping his hands. "Everything went like clockwork."

She felt him looking over her shoulder, and he confirmed it by saying, "Mmmmm," in response to the corned beef casserole she had lingered over. It was one of his attempts to be friendly, she knew, but didn't he know it was rude to look over a person's shoulder? Mother had taught them never to interrupt a person who was in the midst of concentration. Unless your feet were on fire. Didn't Harvey know this?

She flipped a few pages and landed on something called

talarena. "Mmmmm," Harvey said again, then walked on. She was irritated with him for making her move away from the corned beef casserole. She loved corned beef, and this recipe was different from the corned beef pie Mother made, with vegetables and crust and everything. She wasn't ready to try crusts.

The talarena looked good, though, and not too hard. With the cookbook in her hand she started opening the doors of cabinets and refrigerator to see if they had all the ingredients. Ground beef, onion, green pepper, tomatoes, corn, rice, and cheese. They had everything, even the cheddar. Shredded cheddar. She liked the sound of the words. But how did you shred it?

She poked her head into the studio. "Mother. Don't let me interrupt, but how do you shred cheddar?"

"Sweetheart, why don't you ask Harvey?"

"Motherrrr."

Mother sighed and told her how to use the grater to shred the cheese.

Chopping the onions and peppers and shredding the cheese was fun. She thought of Lloyd, who was just learning how to make sandwiches. Consulting the cookbook, she read, "Brown beef, onion, and green pepper in shortening. Simmer for about fifteen minutes, stirring occasionally." The odor of beef, pepper, and onions wafted through her nostrils and made her stomach register empty. It was still a while before dinner. She wished she'd eaten three sandwiches.

"Mmmmm," she said to herself as she occasionally stirred. The casserole had to bake for twenty to thirty minutes, so it should be in the oven by five-thirty. How would she know whether to bake it for twenty minutes or thirty minutes? she wondered.

"Need any help?" Harvey stood tall in the doorway between the kitchen and the dining room. He had silverware in his hands, ready to set the table. What was he doing setting the table on Mother's night? Again he read her question. "We're swapping, since I was running early and she's running late. She's not at a good stopping place."

Oh, Ancil thought. So that's why Mother had told her to ask Harvey. It flustered her, knowing he would be coming in and out while she was in the kitchen. Counting on his absence was why she had chosen Wednesday for her day. She returned to the cookbook, ready to add rice and corn. But the cookbook said cooked rice, and the rice wasn't cooked. She read the back of the rice package to find out how to cook rice. "Uh-oh. Twenty-five minutes," she said aloud before she remembered Harvey was nearby.

"Problems?" he asked. "Can I help?"

Ancil pressed her lips together against responding, against saying anything out loud. No, you can't help, she thought. If I needed help I wouldn't ask you. It was five-fifteen. If the rice had to cook and the casserole had to cook, dinner would be late.

"Let me know if I can help," Harvey said, and he disappeared from view.

Stay there this time, she thought, measuring water into the pan and turning on the burner. She hadn't counted the time for the water to boil before she could add the rice. Thank goodness for the rule about complaining, she thought. The cook was not killed for being late. But next week it would be hamburgers again. They didn't require so much figuring.

Casserole in the oven, she was cutting lettuce for salad when the phone rang. Margaret appeared from nowhere to answer.

"It's for you," Margaret said.

"Me?" Ancil set the lettuce down and reached for a towel to dry her hands. She'd never received a phone call in this house.

"Hello?" she said, making it a question.

"Hey, Ancil. This is Lloyd. Our picture is in the paper."

"What?"

"Our picture is in the paper. The Little Fish. We're in the paper."

Ancil scrunched her face as though he could see it. She was not pleased to be told she was in the paper as a little fish. "What paper?" she asked, hoping no one she knew would read the paper tonight. There was the *Hanover Daily*, which was published every day except Sunday, and Harvey's paper, which came out weekly.

"The *Historian*," he said, "Mama's gone out to buy some extra copies."

Ancil closed her eyes. She didn't tell him she could get

him all the extra copies he wanted. Why had Harvey done that to her? He knew she hated being a little fish. He was the one who'd made her go to the swimming class. He knew she hated it. And now he'd put her picture in the paper.

"I hate being a little fish," she told Lloyd. "I hate having my picture in the paper. Especially *that* paper."

"What's wrong with that paper? I think it's a good paper."

She hung up on his words. She stood in the hall for a minute, trying not to choke on embarrassment and rage. She could see into the kitchen, where the remainder of the pale green lettuce waited to be cut up. The talarena was in the oven, baking, smelling delicious. Harvey was coming in and out of the kitchen carrying glasses full of iced tea, three at a time.

"Just lettuce for salad?" Zan said, coming into the kitchen to see what they were having.

"I've chopped onion, pepper, cheese, and lettuce and that's enough," Ancil said. "If you say one more word, I'll chop your head." Just lettuce was all she could manage with talarena. And if Lloyd had called an hour ago she couldn't have managed talarena.

"Well, pardon me," Zan said. "I don't know who that was who called, but I hope they never call again!"

Ancil slid her hands into the hot mitts, opened the oven door, and carefully lifted the glass dish and carried it into the dining room. She was prepared to holler at Harvey to bring a hot mat, but he already had one on the table.

"Come on, everybody," Zan called. Ancil was grateful for that at least. If she opened her mouth to call everyone to dinner, her anger would come roaring out.

"Mmmmm, looks good," Harvey said, taking his place at one end of the table.

Mother came, sliding out of her painting jacket and hooking it over the back of the chair. "Ancil, why don't you sit at the head of the table?" Mother said. "This looks very special."

Ancil shook her head. If she could keep it attached to her shoulders, she would be doing very well.

"Looks *very* delicious, Ancil," Zan said.

"Mmmmm, yes," said Lydia.

"What's the recipe?" asked Margaret.

Ancil sat at her accustomed place and let the chattering and the passing of food swirl around her.

"Bread, anyone?" Mother said, and a chorus of no-thank-yous rounded the table.

"Mmmmm," said Margaret after she'd blown on a forkful of talarena and put it in her mouth. "What's the recipe?"

This time they noticed Ancil was not responding.

"Ancil?" Mother gave her a questioning look.

"She's going to be one of these cooks who does not divulge the recipe," Harvey said. "I noticed that when I saw her perusing the corned beef recipe she flipped pages and decided on something else."

"Oh, come on," Margaret said. "You're not going to be like that, are you?"

Ancil concentrated on her plate. Mother knew, she thought. Mother knew it was more than the recipe.

"If she doesn't want to share the recipe, that's cook's prerogative," Harvey said.

His big words, his casual tone, his trying to fit in, trying to act as though he belonged here made Ancil feel as though she were being shredded. "Why did you do it!" she said, spitting the words.

Harvey looked astonished.

Lydia said, "Do what? Look over your shoulder at the corned beef recipe?"

"It's nothing to get angry about, really," Margaret said.

"Why did you put my picture in the paper?" She felt her eyes shoot fire, red as her hair, tongues of fire from a dragon's mouth.

Zan and Lydia popped questions. "Your picture's in the paper? Oh, Ancil, isn't that great? Can I have my picture in the paper?"

"It's not enough that I hate being a little fish," Ancil said. "It's not enough that I hate having to live in this house with you. You have to embarrass me in front of all my friends by putting my picture in the paper with a bunch of babies."

Silence had stricken the dining room. Mouths hung open. Forks stopped midway between plates and lips. Margaret started to say something, but Harvey stopped her. Ancil noticed. Big head of household, she thought bitterly.

"It wasn't my decision," Harvey said. "But when I saw it, I thought you'd like it." Margaret again started to say something, but Harvey held up a hand and tipped his head to her.

"I know what you thought I'd like," Ancil said.

"Ancil, stop it," Mother said.

"I know why Margaret or Lyddy or Zan's picture hasn't been in the paper. Or Mother's. You don't have to win them over and you think you can win me over." She pushed back from the table and stood up. "Well, I'll tell you one thing, Mr. Harvey *Hanover Historian* Hutton, there is nothing you can do to win me over." She stepped away from the table and glared at Harvey. "Eat my talarena," she said. "I hope you choke!"

Before she could get past him, he rose from his chair and reached out for her. She dodged. Mother said his name in a cautioning tone and he dropped his hand.

"I think we've done enough catering," Mother said. A couple of "Me, too's" followed. "If there is any winning over, she'll have to do it herself."

Ancil had reached the stairs and knew Mother was speaking loud enough to be sure she heard. "Fat chance!" she said just as loudly, stomping her foot on each stair, flinging herself through the doorway of her room, banging the door shut behind her, and bouncing onto the bed.

Fat chance! She hated that she didn't know some more effective words. Perhaps she should have asked Harvey for a dictionary instead of a parrot.

chapter 8

Ancil stared and glared at the parrot, or where the parrot was, draped in a towel. Even through the towel and with the sun in the west, the colors seemed to sparkle and reproach her. Her strongest impulse was to remove the parrot from its perch and dash it, smash it, or pitch it out the window. Yes. She liked that idea. But even in her fury she knew the outer limit, and she was already almost beyond it.

At any minute it would be lecture time. They would calmly finish dinner, for they were basically a calm family. Then Mother or Harvey or Mother and Harvey would come up to talk. They were so insistent on being reasonable. Why didn't they yell at her, shout at her?

The window. Yes. Throwing the parrot out the window would be such immediate satisfaction. The image of herself going out the window blipped through her mind, but she immediately rejected it. She didn't like the vision of sailing through space and splatting on the ground. Or worse, landing spraddle and speared in the middle of the oleander hedge.

But the window, yes. There was a definite possibility in the window and the trellis, which so neatly climbed the side of the house. When it got dark, she would climb down the trellis, walk west to King Street, then north on King all the way to Juniper. If she appeared in Juniper exhausted and bedraggled from having walked the entire forty miles, they would realize her desperation. Gran and Grandy would hug her and take her in and let her stay. Mother, too, would realize this was best and would want her happiness. Harvey would be relieved to be rid of her.

Involved with her mental meanderings, she forgot she was expecting the lecture until there was a knock on the door. She didn't respond, and the knock was repeated.

"Ancil, it's me, Zan."

Ancil was surprised, but still she didn't answer.

"You're wanted on the phone," Zan said. "It's that boy, Lloyd." Interest and excitement flared enough for Ancil to raise herself to a sitting position, but there she stopped. No, she wasn't leaving her room even to talk to Lloyd. In fact, she didn't want to talk to him. He was the one who was so proud of being a little fish, so proud of having his picture in the paper with a bunch of six-year-olds. From the other side of the door came a loud, exasperated sigh, then receding footsteps. Ancil crossed her legs and arms in smug satisfaction.

After a while there was another knock. Ancil was still sitting Indian fashion, facing the door. She sent go-away thoughts toward it. The knob turned and Zan's head peeked around.

"May I come in?" she asked.

Ancil didn't answer, and Zan came in and shut the door behind her. "I don't understand you any more, Ancil," Zan said. Zan sat on the floor beside the bed and assumed Ancil's crossed arms and legs position. Zan didn't say anything, and Ancil knew Zan was waiting for her to speak. Once they had been soul sisters, sharing their joys and aggravations as well as their room. Best-friend sisters. For this abdication, Ancil thought, Zan was the worst traitor of all. Without consciously making a vow, she realized she had decided not to speak.

"I'm not the one who put your picture in the paper," Zan said finally. "But it wasn't Harvey, either."

The comment disgusted Ancil—all this defense of Harvey.

"It's a good picture, really," Zan said. "Have you even seen it? It doesn't say you're a little fish. It's just a bunch of kids in the pool. Your class. The other classes. Regular swimmers. You know, that back page of photos that's always in the paper."

Ancil didn't know, didn't care, had never looked at the

Hanover Historian reporting history as it happens.

"Anyway, it was Margaret who was in charge of that page this week. It was Margaret who put your picture in the paper."

Margaret?

"She really thought you'd like it."

Margaret?

"You really hurt her feelings."

Margaret. But Margaret hadn't taken the picture. Who had taken the picture? Pain was being added to pain.

"I don't know why you're so hateful to Harvey. You're not giving yourself a chance."

At least that was a twist. What Ancil had heard so often was that she wasn't giving Harvey a chance.

"If you think you're not going to speak to them, don't worry," Zan said. "They're not going to speak to you, either. Mother said there had been enough discussion of the situation and everyone already knew how everyone else felt. She said that if there was any winning over you would have to be the one to do it."

Ancil remained passive. Trying not to think of Margaret. Just trying to survive until Zan decided to leave.

"What's that for?" asked Zan, noticing the wrapped parrot.

Thinking of the parrot and her impulse to throw it out the window made Ancil know what would make Zan leave the room. She spoke.

"I'm thinking of pitching it out the window," she said

with perfect calm. "Along with Margaret's new clothes, Bridey, and *your doll*."

Zan's eyes almost crossed in surprise. But her arms and legs uncrossed and she leaped to her feet. Now she was the speechless one, mouth opening and closing mutely for a moment before she fled. As she flew through the doorway, she regained her vocal chords. "Mother, Mother, do you know what Ancil said?"

Zan left the door open and Ancil felt invaded. Everyone's space was now flooding into her own. But she was immobilized. She would spend her life here on the bed, not speaking.

Lydia appeared at the top of the stairs. Ancil withdrew her eyes. Then Lyddy was in the doorway.

"I won't bother you by talking because I know you don't want to listen," Lyddy said. "I know how I hate it when someone talks and talks when I don't want to listen. I just want to tell you that I love you." Quite rapidly Lydia crossed the room, gave Ancil a hug, and returned to the door. "I think you want your door closed, don't you?" And Lyddy closed the door and left Ancil alone inside.

The closing door was the ripcord on her tear glands. She fell onto her back and tears traced down the sides of her face and wet her hair. But she made no sound.

After a while she realized she was lying in the dark. Dark. Dark was when she was going to run away, climb down the rose trellis and walk all the way to Juniper. She didn't have money for the bus, and she would never try to hitch a ride. Besides, she wanted to walk. All forty miles.

She pushed herself up from the bed. Her face was all damp and her nose dripped onto her upper lip. There were tissues in the bathroom, but she couldn't go there. The only security in the house was here behind this door. She pulled her desk chair under the parrot and wiped her face and nose on the towel. From the height of the chair she looked out the window, past the sheer light blue curtains, which did not show their color in the dark.

She wondered if Mr. Duggan was on his high observation deck and if he could see her. Down from the chair, curtains brushed back from the window, she peered into darkness. If she couldn't see him, then he couldn't see her.

What she should do, she guessed, was have a practice run to be sure climbing down was possible. She would need jeans and a long-sleeved shirt to guard against the rose thorns. And gloves. She lifted her jeans from a peg in the closet, then dug through her drawers and pulled out a red sweatshirt and her gloves, also red.

When she returned to the window, it took her a few minutes to remember the combination to undo the screen. Thanks to Harvey for knowing how to do it at all. One of their chores had been to help clean the screens, and he had shown them how to slide the screens out of the brackets. Once the screen was loose, though, she dropped it. She clenched her teeth and eyes, as though that action would soften the crash. But there was no crash, just a whispered brushing of the oleander hedge and a muffled thud. She waited a minute, and when the falling screen didn't attract any attention, she backed out over the sill.

The shrouded parrot dangled above her. "And don't you dare say a word," she whispered to it.

Since it was dark and she couldn't see down, she wasn't afraid of the height. She bumped her foot around, seeking a toehold on the trellis, pressing her big toe forward in her sneaker. For once she was glad to be lightweight, smaller than Zan. A little fish. Clinging to the sill with hands and arms, she pushed against the trellis with her toe, finding a foothold, testing the support. Then, in one scary move, she transferred her hands from the sill to the sides of the trellis where it came up to the window. An image flickered, of herself falling, whispering past oleanders and landing with a muted thud. Oh, please, she thought. If she fell, she would hope to make enough noise to be heard.

She brushed such thoughts aside. She would not fall. She pretended that there was a fire and this was her only escape. She moved her right foot down a notch, then her left hand. Left foot, right hand. Her heart went *ploomp*. It would work. It was working. She was tempted to scramble back up and leap into the safety of her room, but she calmed herself. She had to make sure she could climb all the way down. Foot, hand, foot, hand, foot, hand. Rose thorns snagged at her clothing, and one pierced her finger through the glove.

All of a sudden there was light from somewhere. She

pressed herself against the trellis and scratched her cheek. It was only a light from the house, from the hallway, shining through the kitchen. She ducked her head and peered in, but there was no one there, no shadows of someone lurking, watching her. If they caught her doing this they would flat-out kill her and she wouldn't have to worry about where to live.

Slowly she eased on down, and when a foot touched ground she poked it around to be sure. Then she backed into the screen and nearly scared the stuffing out of herself. The screen had landed upright against the oleanders.

I made it, she thought. She was so pleased with herself that she cupped a woolen hand over her mouth to contain a whoop. I really could do it, she thought. I really could sneak out and run away. She was amazed and frightened by the freedom of it. It was much more heady than running around the courthouse. She looked up to where she had come from and gulped.

She turned to take a few steps to see how it would feel, and she bumped into the shadowy dark. With a start, she realized she had never been outside in the dark alone. The height of the window and the depth of the dark petrified her. The dark, like ocean water, kept moving; tips of black-fingered waves reached out to grab her and drag her under. A door banged from over at the Duggans'. She leaped to the wall of the house and tried to press herself behind the trellis, but rose thorns kept her out.

All she wanted now was to be back in her room, safe in

her bed. She couldn't imagine being able to climb the rose trellis fast enough! The very thought of climbing made her dizzy. How could she get back inside without climbing the trellis? Mother and Harvey were still up. What would they say if she just rang the front doorbell? What would she say? "I fell out the window"?

With all sorts of terror gripping her, she clutched the trellis and began the climb. "What if I fall" thoughts invaded her again. How long before they would find her body? What a shock it would be for one of them to look out the kitchen window to admire the roses and see her lying there all broken inside her red sweat shirt like a giant fallen rose, or an eagle, a red eagle. Careful hand by careful foot, she made her way to the sill, gripped it, and pulled herself over it.

Weak with relief, she stumbled to the bed, ripped the sheet down, jumped in, and pulled the sheet to her chin. Her heart was beating at her temples, in her neck, her chest, and in her ears. Her entire body was pounding. Damp with anxious sweat, she flung off the sheet, then pulled it up again just to have something to clutch.

The olive shell. She needed the olive shell. She leaped to the dresser and back as though in one motion. Lloyd. He'd had stepfathers. He would understand her feelings. Never mind that Margaret was now mixed up in everything. She thought of Lloyd, so pleased to be a little fish, so happy learning how to swim. She thought of him calling her spaghetti-head and talking about her turquoise eyes. The olive shell had warmed in her hand. Its smoothness and the sharp spiral point were familiar to her touch. Sigh-h-h. She'd done it. She'd actually climbed down the rose trellis. Any night she wanted to, any night she needed to, she could be gone and halfway to Gran's by morning.

The wall of dark pressed against her eyes and reminded her of her on-the-ground fright. She'd never been afraid of the dark before. But all that moving, shadowy dark. Too much dark. If she ran away, she'd have to get used to it. Perhaps she would practice some more, climb down the rose trellis every night until she got used to it. She would pretend something to make her brave, as she'd pretended house afire in order to climb down before.

She would have some noble purpose, climbing down the rose trellis. She would be a super hero, a guardian of the night, catching burglars and car thieves. She thought of her red hair, her red gloves, her red sweat shirt, her red sneakers. She thought of the image of the fallen giant rose and the eagle. That was it. She would call herself Red Eagle. Red Eagle would not be afraid of millions and jillions of miles of dark.

In her imagination eagle wings sprouted at her shoulders. She would not even have to climb down the trellis. Mere Ancil would have to climb down, but Red Eagle would wave good-bye to the parrot and leap from the sill. So, flying, she fell asleep.

chapter 9

Imagination and sleep did wonders. Just knowing she *could* get away helped. She awoke blinking at the sunlight, surprised to find herself still in her clothes—the jeans and sweat shirt. A little guiltily, she slipped out of them and into her nightgown for the trip across the hall to the bathroom.

She cracked her bedroom door and was relieved not to see or hear anyone. She gained the bathroom safely. What would they say to her? If, as Zan had said, they weren't going to speak, that would make it easier.

She splashed her face with cold wake-up water. When she reached up for a towel, a strange image glanced at her from the mirror. Her cheek was bloody from the scratch, which she had forgotten about. Her hand moved quickly to cover it. Thank goodness no one had seen her. How would she explain it?

Washing her face had knocked the scab off, and she dabbed a tissue against the fresh blood. It only bled for a moment, but there was an obvious red line crossing her cheek. The screen had fallen, she remembered, nodding, thinking of an explanation. When she saw the screen had fallen, she would say, she had leaned out to see what had happened and she had scratched her face on a rose thorn. Of course, if she wasn't talking, she wouldn't have to give an explanation.

Back in her room, she went to the window to see if there was a thorn close enough to have scratched her. There was not. The roses were up along one side of the window, however. She carefully grabbed a stem between thorns, yanked it loose from the trellis, and pulled it in front of the window. When she let it go, it returned to its position. At least it was loose, and it could have been in front of the window.

There below was the screen, still standing upright against the oleanders. The screen, having flown from the window, made her remember Red Eagle. She smiled. No one in the world would know that Ancil Witherspoon was Red Eagle.

In the hall as they were both heading for the stairs, she ran into Zan.

"What happened to your face?" Zan asked. When Ancil

didn't answer, Zan followed with, "Are you speaking to us this morning?" Well, obviously, Zan was speaking, Ancil noted. "Suit yourself," Zan said, and scuttled down the stairs. Red Eagle came after.

The two of them put out cereal, milk, and juice in the kitchen. Mother wandered in, holding a cup of tea.

"What happened to your face?" she asked.

"She's not speaking," Zan said.

"Zan, let Ancil speak for herself," Mother said.

"She's not speaking," Zan repeated.

Mother and Ancil looked at each other, but Ancil didn't speak. She turned back to pouring cereal, milk, and juice.

"Is that the way you're going to be?" Mother asked.

Ancil didn't look up this time. A stubborn amusement circled around somewhere inside. She was no longer angry, just filled with determination.

"Well, suit yourself," Mother said.

Suit yourself, suit yourself, Ancil thought. They must have had a family conference and decided to let her suit herself. Well, she would.

"Did you put disinfectant on that scratch?" Mother asked. Ancil had not. "If you didn't, be sure to. It could get infected."

Now Margaret came in. "Your friend Lloyd was at the Duggans' last night," she said. "He's cute. I like him. You should have come over." Margaret reached into a cabinet for a bowl and set about preparing her cereal.

Ancil was surprised at the mention of Lloyd. If she'd

been talking she would have had to say, "Oh, Margaret, re-eally," as though the thought of Lloyd's being cute had never entered her mind.

As they both spooned cereal, Zan and Margaret chattered about day camps and newspaper offices. If Margaret's feelings were still hurt, she wasn't showing it.

Upstairs, Ancil dabbed some alcohol on her scratch.

Bathing suit and towel dangling from her hand, she was almost at the Rec Park before it dawned on her that she had not even considered not coming. The thought stopped her, halfway across the green space. Probably they would have made her come, and probably she had had sense enough to know that. Until she could leave, she would at least act cooperative. Except for speaking.

Lloyd hailed her. She watched him angle across from the entrance columns at Whitaker Street. His hair had lightened from sun and swimming, and his body had tanned. He *was* cute, she thought, so bronze and boxy.

"You should have been there last night. At Duggans'. I learned four stars and four constellations," he said, and listed them. "That's what I called you about. I was going over to look through the telescope. I wanted you to come." He walked along beside her, babbling on, not giving her a chance to speak. During his monologue she remembered her resolve of silence. Should she include him? "You should see what you can see through a telescope. Millions and billions of stars. Your sister Margaret came over. She says you've never come. Why not?"

He was walking jauntily, outstepping her with his long strides, then stopping, turning toward her for a moment before stepping along with her again.

"When you wouldn't come to the phone, your sister said you were mad at having your picture in the paper. Gosh, I loved having my picture in the paper. Who cares if it's with some little fish? I don't know why that bothers you so much. Aren't you glad to be learning how to swim?" He tilted his head and looked at her, puzzled.

"Mama has promised to take me to the ocean when I get my certificate," he said.

She had decided that she would keep her silence with him, too. If she talked to him, she might forget and talk at home. Now he noticed. He stopped walking and stared at her. "Are you mad at me?" His voice rose to a high note. "I didn't put your picture in the paper, so why would you be mad at me about it? I just called to tell you 'cause I thought you'd be happy about it."

Now he was mad, she thought. Funny how anger multiplied itself. When someone was mad at someone else, the someone else being mad at also got mad. Perhaps with him she should talk.

"If you're going to go around being mad, then I'll be back to having no friends again," he said. He didn't sound at all mad, just a little sad. Wasn't he mad at her for being mad at him? She was surprised at his reaction, pleased he wasn't mad. She pointed to her mouth to signal she wasn't mad but just wasn't talking.

"Oh? You're not mad?" His face shone. "You have laryngitis?"

She shook her head but kept pointing to her mouth.

"You don't have laryngitis? What, then?"

She kept shaking and pointing until his expressions changed.

"Oh, I get it," he said. "You're just not talking." She nodded, and he smiled. "Is that why you didn't come to the telephone?" She nodded. "Between the first time I called and the second time I called you decided to stop talking?" They were near the pool gate, and he paused to complete the conversation before going within earshot of the people around the pool.

She nodded again. She hadn't exactly decided not to talk; it had just sort of happened. But there was no way she could explain that unless she spoke.

He was smiling and shaking his head. "You mean you haven't said a word since last night?" He seemed amused and amazed.

She hadn't thought it out, about how she was not going to speak or to whom she was not going to speak. So here she was with this unthought-out commitment to silence. How long would she last? she wondered.

"Then that's another thing you're good at, Ancil. Sometimes I think I won't speak for a while, but I always forget. I don't last thirty minutes."

The sixth-graders were not guarding the gate, so Ancil didn't have to confront Marcia. If she wasn't talking, there'd be no confrontation, anyway. She was pleased that not talk-ing could be so beneficial.

In the pool Lloyd was on his own, doing laps across the center between the rescuers and the little fish.

"Hey, you'll be in our class in no time," she heard Shafer say. She paddled back and forth with the little ones, doing better but still not nearly as well as most of them were doing. When the lesson was over and she was dressed, there was Marcia, blocking the gate.

"Cram it, huh?" Marcia said. "You told me to cram it, didn't you, you little plate of spaghetti."

Spaghetti? Lloyd had gotten them all started, she thought. Noodle would be next. She walked as though she were going through the gate, but Marcia didn't move.

"You have a big mouth for such a scrawny kid," Marcia said. "Too bad your feet are stuck in your mouth, otherwise you'd race with me."

"Yeah, do it," Lloyd said. "You can beat her." Ancil hadn't seen him come out of the dressing room.

"I doubt that," Marcia said. "I doubt that very much."

"I don't," Lloyd said.

"I thought you were our friend," Shafer said to Lloyd.

"I'm Ancil's friend best of all," Lloyd said.

"Okay, Shafer, Marcia. Move out of the way and let them go by." This was Kirby.

"Make me," Marcia said, glaring at Kirby. Kirby shrugged, looking apologetically at Lloyd but not at Ancil.

She could see they'd be here all day, trying to get Marcia

to move from the gate. She knew she could leave Marcia in her dust. Suddenly she nodded, indicating she would race. That would at least remove Marcia from the gate.

"Do you mean you'll race?" Shafer asked, revved up with excitement.

"Do you mean you'll race?" Lloyd repeated.

Their enthusiasm irritated Ancil. What was this excitement about physical things—baseball, swimming, racing? What about multiplication tables?

"She won't race," Marcia said. "She's chicken." Ancil kept nodding to indicate her willingness to race. "What's all this waggly-head business?" Marcia asked.

"She's not talking," Lloyd said.

"Not talking?" Kirby repeated.

"Big deal," said Shafer.

"High and mighty 'cause she had her picture in the paper with all the little fish," Marcia said. "Just because it's her father's newspaper."

"Your father's newspaper?" Lloyd asked. He's not my father, Ancil thought. The words roared within her, but she could not say them. She was bound to silence.

"She's your friend and you didn't know that?" Shafer said. "Some friend."

"Little fish, little fish," Marcia said, but she still didn't move from the middle of the gate. Ancil pulled her lips between her teeth and held them tightly to keep from shouting. She nodded vigorously, wanting to race, wanting Marcia away from blocking the gate. Red Eagle would be at Princess Avenue before Marcia got halfway across. She leaned into a racer's pose for emphasis.

"Does that mean you'll race?" Marcia asked.

Didn't they know anything? Was she going to have to shake her head off before they caught on?

"Alllll right!" Shafer said. "I'll go across and hold my arms out and you race to me."

"I'll be the starter," Kirby said.

"Go, Ancil, go!" Lloyd said.

"The starting place will be right here from the edge of the sidewalk," Kirby said, moving to the place. The sidewalk crossed toward the tennis courts and the Little League ball fields.

Shafer jogged across the grass, stopped, and turned, and at last Marcia moved away from the gate. Shafer waggled his arms. "Marcia," he called, moving his left arm. "Ancil." He waggled his right.

Shaking her head, amazed at herself for taking part in this spectacle, Ancil hunched into a starting position next to Marcia.

"Ready?" Kirby asked. "Ready, set, go!"

Feet flying, elbows pumping, Ancil sprinted off well ahead of Marcia. She knew she was the faster one. This was too easy—what did she have to prove? She slowed a bit until Marcia was in her peripheral vision, at her shoulder. Then she slowed a bit more and let Marcia pull ahead. Lloyd was screaming to give her speed, but she slowed to a walk and headed out toward Princess Avenue. If Marcia wanted to be faster, let Marcia be faster, Ancil thought. She ran as fast as she ran, and what else mattered?

Halfway to Shafer, Marcia looked over her shoulder and saw Ancil walking away. She stopped, held out her hand, and began to yell. "Little chicken fish, I knew you wouldn't race."

But I got you to move from the gate, didn't I? Ancil thought.

"Little fish, little fish, little fish."

The catcalls made her feelings flipflop. Now she wished she'd run like the wind, like Red Eagle, and left Marcia in her dust. But she kept walking, kept ignoring calls of "Little fish" at her back. Then, "Turtle."

"Hey, Ancil, wait up," Lloyd called, but she didn't wait. "Wait up," he called again.

Who cares? she thought. Maybe she wasn't Lloyd's friend. Maybe he wasn't hers. But who cares? Being mad did multiply. When she was mad at someone, it made it easier to be mad at everyone else. But what did it matter? Soon, soon she would have these awful weeks in Hanover behind her and she would slice them out of her memory as though they had never been. She would do it. She would figure some way to do it.

"Now why did you do that?" Lloyd said when he caught up. She didn't answer, of course. "That's right, you're not speaking. I forgot. Ancil, I just don't understand you."

It was frustrating, not talking. If she were talking, she would have returned question for question. Why had he been strike-out king at school when he could hit better than anyone else? She didn't understand him. Did he think he was the only one who didn't understand things? And they'd had this conversation before.

She pantomimed swinging the bat, holding fingers up to indicate one, two, three strikes.

"Okay, okay," he said. "I get it."

chapter 10

Lloyd and Ancil parted at the side street that went down to Whitaker, near Lloyd's house. The striped stray cat was on the sidewalk, and she watched it scamper away when he tried to coax it to him. His mother wouldn't let him come to lunch two days in a row. Ancil was a little disappointed, but it was okay. Her friendship with Lloyd would be short, anyway, if she moved back to Juniper.

As she walked on behind the school, she began noticing houses. Some of the houses were twins, painted differently but having the same combination of porches, windows, and turrets. Harvey had pointed it out on that first Hanover tour, but she'd been so busy ignoring him that she hadn't seen much. Grand Square had been gloriously in bloom, with dogwoods and azaleas. The tour, she guessed afterward, was supposed to soften them for the big announcement.

Had she really never noticed that pink house with green shutters? Who would have ever thought of such a combination? But it was lovely, really. The pink was pale and the green contrasted but didn't shout. The walk with Lloyd yesterday had helped her begin to see. Hanover, she admitted, wasn't such a bad town.

Happier than she had thought she could be on this day after such a rupturing outburst, she went into the house, and there was Harvey, crossing the hall.

"Hi, uh, Ancil. Can I make you lunch?" he asked. "I was just on my way to the kitchen."

She'd forgotten. It was Thursday. His day off.

"Bologna? How about a fat bologna sandwich with lettuce, tomato, onion, and pickle?"

She walked directly to the stairway and started up. She would have lunch later when he was through in the kitchen.

"Ancil, I love you," he said. The words bounced off her back and helped push her up the stairs. In the bathroom she hung the sodden towel and bathing suit over the rim of the tub. She knew he loved her, or knew he said he loved her. But didn't he know it was perfectly possible to love someone who doesn't love you back? Like Lloyd and that striped cat. Why were they all so determined to ignore her feelings?

In her room she took the picture of Dad off the dresser. She propped herself against the headboard of the bed with the picture against her knees. Hanover or Juniper wasn't the point. The point was that she had a father, Mother had a husband, and it was supposed to be the same person. Daddy. Alexander Witherspoon.

She stared at the picture. Daddy was twenty-three in this picture. He and Mother had married right after high school, when they were eighteen. Both families had had a fit, their marrying so young. Mother's family had moved away, thinking she would come with them. Mother stayed and married Daddy. Gran and Grandy had sent Dad to college, as they had planned. Margaret and Lydia were born right away. Dad graduated and joined the Air Force to keep from having to go into the army. They'd bought the little house, and Mother had stayed in Juniper while Daddy went here and there and yonder. Soon after Ancil was born, he was sent to Vietnam.

A motion caught her eye, and involuntarily she looked up. Harvey was at the door, leaning his tall self against the frame, filling the doorway. She hadn't heard him come up the stairs.

"Someone once said we should learn to live with one another without hurting or dwarfing each other," he said. "And, Ancil, you're hurting me."

After the involuntary glance she returned her eyes to the picture. She examined her father, his hair whorling in cowlicks at the front, just like on the sculpture and now on the mask. You're hurting me, too, she thought.

"I know I'm hurting you, too," he said, "but I don't mean to." How, she wondered, was he always able to respond to her unspoken comments or questions? "I can't do all the giving, Ancil. You have to give, too. I don't want to replace your father in your affection or in your memory. He is a lucky, lucky man to have you love him so fiercely."

He paused. She hated the pauses adults put into their speeches. She waited, miserable, for him to go on, to get finished and leave her doorway.

"But your father is not here, Ancil, and I am. I do want to be a father to you. A second father. Fathers often have more than one child and they love them equally. Why can't a child have more than one father?" Another pause. "Ancil, we have to do something to stop the hurting."

She studied her thumbs where they touched the sides of the picture frame. She felt the balls of each of her fingers as they pressed against the back of the picture. Her eyes went moist in acknowledgment of the hurting, but she knew there was nothing to stop it—unless Daddy came home.

"Ancil, damn it," Harvey said, taking long strides and stalking into her room. She recoiled at his words, at his movement, and drew her knees to her chest with the picture closeted in between. His huge hands came at her. With one hand he grasped the edge of the picture and wrenched it from her. With the other he took one of hers and dragged her off the bed.

"Ancil, damn it, I have pictures, too!" He set the picture of Daddy on the dresser and pulled her skidding from the room. With her free hand she plucked futilely at his grip on her. In Mother and Harvey's room, without releasing her hand, he opened the bottom drawer of his dresser, reached under some clothes, and drew out a packet of pictures. He pushed her down in a chair and stood above her, trapping her there.

"You're not the only one who has pictures," he said, thrusting pictures in her face, almost too close for her to see. A blond-haired woman and two blond-haired little girls smiled out at her. The woman and children were sometimes together, sometimes separate, in doorways, in high chairs, on tricycles. Ancil knew the story. They'd all three been killed in a car accident eight or so years ago. She was sorry. Sorry.

"See? See? See?" Harvey said as he flipped through the pictures, not looking at them himself. Finally he removed the pictures from her face, dropped his arm, and stood there. He seemed to be as stunned by his behavior as she was. In a moment he raised his arm and held the pictures in front of himself. He seemed lost, as though he had entered into the pictures.

Ancil shrank against the chair, wanting release, waiting for him to come back and release her. He stood staring blankly over her head, and she was terrified of what he might say next.

She leaped up, shouting. "But they're dead! You know they're dead. My father is not dead!"

She fled to her room, slammed the door, and fell on the

bed, smothering her face in the pillow. She was desperate again. She would run away, she decided. She really would. Tonight.

In her mind she repeated the climb down the rose trellis. She remembered the awesome depth of the dark. Well, I'll practice, she thought. She had no need to practice climbing down the trellis. She already knew she could do that. What she needed was to learn the yard and the street so she would know them in the dark.

She saw neither Mother nor Harvey as she slipped out the front door and hopped over the rail to the side yard. The side yard was very narrow and there was a corridor between the house and the oleander hedge. If she stayed close to the house, she noted, there was nothing to bump into or stumble over. Back to the house, palms pressed flat against it, she slid along the passage. She closed her eyes to make it dark. Her head was below the windows, even without ducking. Yes, she decided, this would work very well.

As she sidled along with her eyes closed, voices from above startled her. She jerked around and looked up, but the voices were not for her.

"Won't that be giving in?" Mother was asking.

"Well, yes, in a way, Laura, but she has to have some breathing room."

They were talking about her. Ancil backed against the house and almost took the form of the wood.

"And you," Mother asked. "Do you need breathing room?"

"No," he said. "Well, yes, but not as much. This is my house, and she doesn't really feel like it's hers yet. She's just now letting herself grieve, and that takes a while. You and I know that."

Ancil wanted to peep. She wanted to see where they were in relation to each other—sitting, standing, touching, apart? But the windows were too high, and if they weren't, Mother and Harvey might see her. What were they planning? she wondered.

"I love you so much," Ancil heard Mother say.

"Mmmm, and I you," Harvey said.

Now Ancil knew, just as clearly as if she could see. They were standing. They were hugging.

"I just wish Ancil could love you," Mother said. "She doesn't know what she's missing."

Ancil clamped her teeth and squinched her eyes shut and resumed sliding along the house until the trellis stopped her. She knew what she was missing. It was Daddy she was missing. Yet she knew Mother had missed Daddy just as fiercely. Even with work and all the children, Mother had missed Daddy so much. And Daddy probably never would—no, she couldn't even think it. Why couldn't she be like Margaret and Zan and Lyddy? Why couldn't she be happy about Harvey? Harvey was not like the invisible rabbit. He would not disappear. But he wasn't like Bluebeard, either; he wouldn't chop off anyone's head.

She heard her name called in the distance. Mother was calling upstairs to her. She jumped and ran as though she had done something wrong. There was no law she had to be in her room. That was just where they thought she was. She opened the back door and stomped to announce herself. Since she wasn't talking, she couldn't call out, "Here I am."

"Oh, there you are," Mother said. "Telephone."

Ancil crossed her arms and stopped six feet from where the phone receiver was hooked over the side of the wall phone.

"Suit yourself," Mother said. "It's Gran. I'll tell her you're not talking." Mother reached for the phone but Ancil grabbed it first, cradling it for a moment before she said hello.

"How's my little conspirator?" Gran asked.

"Okay," Ancil said, dragging the word out and making it sound dreary.

"I know it's Zan's turn to come be the special, but I need some help finishing my project and you're the only one who knows what I'm doing. If I come for you tomorrow after swimming lessons, will you come home with me for the weekend?"

"Of course," Ancil said, making up her mind she would never come back to Hanover.

"I'll make it up to Zan later," Gran said. "In fact, I have another project, too. We'll be very busy. You might not have much time to run around and see your friends."

Her friends would be back from the Washington trip by now, Ancil thought. She wasn't sure she wanted to spend a lot of time with them anyway, listening to them talk about the trip. "That's okay," she said. "You know how I like to help you in the studio."

When she hung up, she was a little deflated and also puzzled. How could she possibly not be enthusiastic about going to Juniper? Partly it was because she knew they must have some plan. And partly, yes, partly it was because she'd been robbed of her own plan. Upstairs she stood under the shrouded parrot, looking out the window. She wouldn't be climbing down the rose trellis. Instead, Gran was coming after her. Idly she raised the window and reached for the rose stem she had pulled loose this morning. Poor Red Eagle. Even before the first adventure, Red Eagle was dead.

chapter 11

All the rest of Thursday Ancil maintained her silence. The family chattered on and included her in conversations as though she were taking part. Not even Zan made any remarks about Ancil's not talking, as though it were the norm.

They talked of day camp and animals, painting and newspapers, and Margaret talked about stars and Donnie Duggan. It was enough to make Ancil glad she wasn't talking. She wouldn't want to talk about swimming lessons, couldn't talk about the totem poles, and she didn't think they would be impressed that she knew her fourteen tables.

That night, as she packed a few things for Gran's, she heard voices from the Duggans' deck. She stepped to the window and looked across, but she couldn't see anything. Her window was open, and the screen had been replaced. She recognized Margaret's voice, and there was another high voice, too. Had Zan or Lydia gone over? Or was it Lloyd? For a wishful moment she was sorry she was not with them.

On her way to swimming lessons Friday morning, she met Lloyd waiting for her on Princess Avenue.

"I saw you last night," he said.

"You saw me? Where?" His words startled words out of her, though neither of them noticed for a minute.

"Standing at your window," he said. "I was on the Duggans' deck."

It *was* him, then, she thought. And while she was looking out her window thinking of him, he was looking over, thinking of her.

"You're talking," he said.

She hadn't realized it herself until he said so. She was almost ready to resume silence, but decided, why not talk to him? This was Lloyd, after all, not Harvey, not Mother, not Lyddy, not Zan or Margaret. "Well, I'm talking to you, anyway," she said.

Shouts of "Little fish, little fish, tu-u-urtle," greeted them long before they reached the pool gate. Marcia, Bobby, Shafer were yelling out the words.

Lloyd nudged Ancil. "We both won't talk to them," he said, and together they ran the gauntlet of words.

In the pool Ancil realized she was beginning to feel at ease swimming on top of the water as well as below it. She could make it all the way across the pool without too much sputtering. Lloyd practiced various strokes the instructor had taught him. He really would be in the other class soon, Ancil thought.

At the end of the lesson, the instructor surprised everyone, most of all Lloyd. Lloyd was awarded his certificate a week early. Lloyd turned pink, rose, carmine, and crimson. All the little fish shouted and clapped, and Ancil clapped loudest.

Holding the certificate out from his body so as not to get it wet, Lloyd whispered to Ancil, "Now Mama will have to take me to the beach. She promised."

When they emerged from the dressing room, Marcia was again blocking the gate.

"Little chicken fish," Marcia said.

Ancil wished she could plow right through her. Gran would be waiting.

"You won't race," Marcia said.

"I'll race," Ancil said, sorry to waste words on Marcia, but she didn't have time for pantomimes, especially since they were so slow to catch on.

"Oh, sure, that's what you said yesterday," Marcia said.

"Okay, I won't," Ancil said, wondering what she could say to make Marcia feel challenged enough to move out of the way.

"Will you? Will you really this time? I don't think little chicken fish can run."

"I'll run," Ancil said. Would she ever run! She would leave Hanover in a burst of speed.

"Let's see if she will," Shafer said, and he crossed the park to what he thought was a good distance, moving toward Princess Avenue this time, as though that would trap her, she thought.

Kirby said, "Ready, set, go."

Ancil sprinted off, flying not like the wind but like an eagle. Red Eagle. Locked into her own Ancil stride, running at her own pace, she never even looked back to see where Marcia was.

"Wow!" came Kirby's and Lloyd's exclamations from behind her.

Shafer looked disappointed when she slapped his outstretched hand.

". . . off to a bad start." She heard Marcia making excuses.

"Wait up," Lloyd called, but Ancil didn't slow down. She just kept running in her own direction and left them all behind. Her side was in stitches, and she was gasping for breath by the time she ran onto the porch at Harvey's. Sweat poured from her as though she were melting. But Gran was there, and it was worth it.

"Goodness gracious!" Gran said. "You are anxious to come home with me, aren't you?"

Ancil nodded, not explaining the other reason for the speed. She pounded up the stairs, grabbed the small straw satchel, and kissed Mother good-bye.

"This heat, I declare," Gran said, touching Ancil's red face.

"It happens every year," Mother said, laughing. "See you Sunday."

Sunday, Sunday, Ancil thought. I won't come home on Sunday. Her wishes were being fulfilled without having to run away. She'd make it work out. Somehow she'd make it work out.

In the car she waited for Gran to start talking about Harvey. How are you and Harvey getting along? Gran would ask, starting out casually. But Gran didn't talk about Harvey. Gran talked about the totems and what still had to be done. And they sang together, harmonizing. "Water on my side, water on my side."

As they topped the stairs at Ancil's grandparents' house, Gran said, "Put your things in Uncle Ran's room. We're going to redecorate the other one. It hasn't been done over for almost twenty years. It needs a new color, don't you think? Yellow, maybe?"

Ancil was struck more speechless than she'd been these past two days. Redecorating? It was as though Gran had sliced out Ancil's tongue. A new color? She stood in the doorway of her father's room. Blue, she thought. It has to be blue. Baby blue, cerulean, royal, navy. Blue. It has always been blue. Her eyes wandered over the pale blue walls. The walls did not want another color, she thought. They wanted to be blue. She looked at the navy quilted drapes and bedspread with their purple haze of time.

She found her tongue, formed words, but her voice sounded as though it were coming from a tunnel. "Oh, no, Gran. No!" She knew, even from the tunnel, that it was useless to say the words. Her grandparents, her father's own parents, had joined the conspiracy to make her stop thinking about her father.

Gran confirmed it. She reached out and grasped Ancil's shoulder and hugged and patted. "It's time, sweetheart. It's way past time."

With everything else in her life so foreign, she could not let her grandparents' house become unfamiliar. "The ship," she said, staring through the doorway at the elaborate model.

"Oh, the ship will stay right where it is," Gran said.

"How old was he when he built the ship?" She was still lost in the labyrinth of her head. They had told her many times when he had built the ship, but she needed to hear recognizable words. How could she be the special in Uncle Ran's room? All through the years when she had walked down the block to spend the night with her grandparents, she had slept in her father's room.

Before she knew where they were going, they were on their way to buy paint.

"I want you to choose the color," Gran said.

"Blue," Ancil said.

"Not blue," Gran said. "Any other color you want— crimson, damson, citron, chartreuse—but not blue."

In the store Ancil became mute again. The colors of paint reminded her of the parrot. All lovely, but she hated them.

When she wouldn't help choose, Gran chose ivory and pale yellow.

"I think maybe burnt sienna for the spread and throw rug and a bright turquoise for throw pillows and the chair. The color of your eyes. What do you think?"

Ancil thought she wanted to stomp and scream. She wanted to ask why everyone was so determined to erase every trace of her father.

"I'd like for you to have a say-so," Gran said. Ancil said nothing. She felt she was being forced to retreat into silence, even with Gran. Again she was overwhelmed with the necessity to run away, but where would she run if not to Gran?

Back home they went into the studio. At least Gran was not going to push through with the painting right this minute. Harvey had said she needed breathing room. She guessed that Gran, too, knew she needed breathing room.

The studio work table was filled with cylinders, now superimposed with masks and designs.

"Some of them are already bisqued," Gran said. "And I want to glaze and fire your family's sections so we can take them over on Sunday."

Sunday. She'd just arrived, and there was already a rush to take her back. Ancil began looking at the totem sections. There was Lydia's face with Bridey and the kittens and various other animals circling the cylinder. There was Aunt Cath with musical notes and a wavery piano keyboard orbiting the section from ear to ear. A slide rule, triangle, T square, and model ship surrounded Grandy. And there was Daddy, with model ship, four little girls, and the date of his disappearance.

"Oh, Gran, they're wonderful," Ancil said as she continued looking. She was eager to find her own, to see how Gran had personalized her. And there she was, her own smooth mask face together with two girls playing hopscotch. She and Jennifer! There was also a stylized sun.

"What's the sun for?" she asked.

"For your sunny disposition," Gran said. "And with that hair, you look like sunshine."

Ancil smiled, feeling complimented but also knowing she hadn't been so sunny lately.

Gran picked up on her thought. "Oh, you'll get it back. You'll see."

I don't know how, Ancil thought, but she didn't say it. With even Gran against her, it was hopeless. As she continued examining the sections, Gran began glazing. Suddenly Ancil was confronted with Harvey.

"Oh, Gran, no!" she said spontaneously. She looked again to be sure, but there he was, staring out from one of the drum shapes with letters like newspaper type scattered around him. When had Gran done Harvey's mask? She looked to see what else depicted Harvey, and there on the same section, surrounded by tubes of paint and paintbrushes, was Mother.

"No, Gran, no!" Ancil cried, and she ran out of the studio.

There was no mention of Harvey or her desertion at the supper table. It was Gran's day to cook, and they had lasagna. Grandy talked about the glass house out in the country by the pond, and Gran said she'd finished glazing the sections for Ancil's family totem. After dinner both Gran and Grandy went up to start painting Daddy's room. They asked Ancil to come, but they didn't insist. Ancil stayed downstairs and watched television.

Sleeping in Uncle Ran's room was strange. The colors were shades of brown and green. One wall was papered with life-size bamboo stalks that looked as though they were growing up the wall. Margaret and Lydia and maybe even Zan had slept here when all four of them had spent the night at once. But she had always been in Daddy's room. This room had been done over sometime before Ancil could remember, when both Dad and Uncle Ran had been grown and married. Dad's room had been left for his return from Vietnam, even though this was no longer the house he would come to.

In the morning, over breakfast, Gran and Grandy talked about shopping for a new bedspread and curtains for the room. Ancil poked at her cereal with the spoon, pushing each floater into the milk.

"We want you to come with us," Gran said.

"We want you to help," Grandy said.

Ancil continued playing with her cereal.

"It's important to all of us," Grandy said. "Believe me, we know what you're feeling."

"Everyone has abandoned Daddy," she said to her bowl.

"I know," Gran said.

"Ancil, sweetheart, it's been ten years. More than ten years." This was Grandy. "Eleven years. My God, it's more than eleven years. But we are not forgetting, and we're not letting our government forget. But it's past time to let your mother forget a little. And you, too."

"No," she said, shaking her head vigorously. Her hair swung across her chin.

"Ancil, you have to acknowledge that your father is probably dead," Grandy said. "Alex is probably dead." Grandy stared into space the way Harvey had two days ago.

He'd said it. How dare he say it, Ancil thought. She knew it, she knew it, but she didn't want to know it. One sob jerked out of her, and she sucked it back, determined not to cry. She thought of reminding them about the occasional news reports that said some of the Missing In Action were thought to be alive. But she couldn't say it. If she said one word she would not be able to hold back her tears.

"Sweetheart, we've been over this so many times. MIA or not, in Georgia, when a person has been missing for seven years, he is presumed dead," Gran said. She reached out and touched Ancil's arm. "Alex—your father—was such a vibrant, lively person. You have a lot of his spunk and spirit. He would not want you to put this part of your life in suspension for so long, believe me. How long should your mother have to wait for a husband? How long should you have to wait to have a father? I mean a real one, who eats breakfast and dinner with you, not one who lives only inside your head."

"You are old enough to have some responsibility toward the family," Grandy said.

Ancil washed the breakfast dishes, slowly, elaborately, delaying, delaying. But they would not leave without her. She followed, solemn, as they trooped through several stores in search of burnt sienna bedspreads.

"Look," Gran said, pleased to have found both the bedspread and the turquoise pillows. Gran held a pillow beside Ancil's face, comparing the color to Ancil's eyes.

"Perfect," Grandy said.

Back home, Ancil sat listlessly in the room, in the worn blue chair that would soon be sent out to be recovered. One on each side, Gran and Grandy remade the bed, then hung the new drapes. The yellow walls looked bright and sunshiny, but Ancil, in spite of having a sun on her totem, did not feel shiny.

Gran's words. Grandy's words. Mother's words, Harvey's words, even Zan's, Lydia's, and Margaret's words from the last few months. Love, responsibility, ten years—no, eleven—none of that mattered except love for Daddy and his love for all of them. How could they know he wouldn't come home? He was missing, not dead. Grandy was wrong. Daddy *was* alive.

For the first time in her life she was hating this house, hating it just as much as she hated the house in Hanover,

She had intended to plead for an extension, to try to stay here forever, but now she didn't care. One place was just as hurtful as the other. There was nothing left of Daddy except the picture, the ship, and the memories inside her head.

chapter 12

Zan, Lyddy, Margaret, Mother, Harvey all clamored to know what was in the newspaper-wrapped items Gran, Grandy, and Ancil were carrying into the house. As Gran began to unwrap them, exclamations of delight filled the air.

"Oh, look! Look at me!" Zan said, studying her face surrounded by replicas of her doll collection, including her newest—the dumpling doll.

"And me!" said Margaret, whose totem included three Margarets in modeling poses, plus several hearts, and the initials MW/EB in the corners of a plus sign. "EB, who's EB?" she asked.

"Everybody," Gran said. "You're a people lover."

"Every Boy," Zan said quickly.

"It's not just boys I like," Margaret said with a see-there-smarty tone. "I like people."

"Especially if they're boys," Zan said. Margaret reached out to swat Zan, but Zan ducked and dodged.

When Harvey spotted his mask there on the same section as Mother's he hugged Gran and said, "Thanks." Ancil pretended not to notice.

When everyone had thoroughly examined each section, Grandy produced some glue. There were more exclamations as everyone realized the pieces were to be put together.

"A totem pole!" Lydia said.

The bottom section had four faces—Gran, Grandy, Dad, and Mother. Onto it was set the one of Harvey and Mother. Then Margaret, Lydia, Ancil, and Zan were stacked and glued in order of age, oldest to youngest.

"My, how you've grown," Harvey said to Zan's mask face, which was suddenly up there almost as tall as his real one.

"And you've shrunk," Zan said, giggling at Harvey's totem below her knees.

Lydia admired Bridey and the kittens on her cylinder. "The real kittens have their eyes open," she said. "Come see." So they tromped upstairs to admire the kittens for a while.

Then Gran said, "I'm ready to put my toes in saltwater," and they tromped down again.

Ancil sighed. She didn't want to go to the beach. But

they always went to the beach when Gran and Grandy came. Going to the beach was a Witherspoon habit. In the back seat of the station wagon with Lyddy and all the picnic stuff, some delicious aroma attacked her nose and hollowed her stomach.

"What's that smell?" she asked. "Fried chicken?" It had been ages since Mother had prepared a fried chicken picnic.

"No mere sandwiches today," Harvey said. "Today is a banquet."

Lyddy pointed up front toward the driver's seat. Ancil frowned, not understanding the motion. "He fixed," Lyddy said. Ancil continued frowning. She thought of Harvey trying so hard to fit himself into the family, taking his turn cooking and everything else. And now he was permanently affixed near the base of the totem pole as though he were part of the foundation of the family. Worrisome thoughts nagged at her. She kept seeing the faces of his little girls, but the image of his wife, his first wife, wouldn't come to mind. What came to mind, quite unbidden, was Mother. Harvey's wife was Mother.

Ancil stared out the window at the verdant marsh. It was bisected by the dark straight causeway and the sparkling curves of tidal creeks. Harvey was her stepfather. Her sisters called him Daddy. He called them honey, darling, sweetheart. His dark hair was like Margaret's, Gran's, and Grandy's. She was surprised she hadn't noted that before. She looked at but did not see the horizon rimmed with the dark green border of trees that marked Golden Isle.

At the beach, with each of them carrying something—basket, blanket, thermos, Frisbee, towels—they topped the boardwalk over the dunes. Even from this distance the sight of the endlessly moving water made Ancil queasy. Deciding on a spot, Mother, Harvey, and Grandy each snapped a blanket into the air. The beach breeze whipped the blankets about like enormous flags; then, like parachutes, each floated onto the sand.

"Last one in is a rotten egg," Grandy said as his blanket settled. He and Zan and Lydia raced to the water. Mother and Gran weighted the corners of the blankets with picnic paraphernalia and sat. Margaret stood looking up and down the beach, examining random groups of people who dotted the sand. Ancil smiled to herself. Margaret, she thought, was looking for "everybody." She herself turned her back to the sea and stared toward the dunes, wondering what to do.

"Would you like to use the binoculars?" Harvey asked, holding them over Ancil's shoulder. Automatically her head jerked sideways in refusal. He'd made the offer before, on other days. Everyone else in the family had learned to use the field glasses, learned to adjust the lenses to the particular eye.

Without changing her head shake to a nod, she reached for the glasses. Having them would give her a reason to stay away from the water. As Harvey gave them to her, he lifted the strap over her head and let it settle against the back of her neck.

"Keep the strap around your neck at all times," he said. "That way, if you drop them, they won't fall."

Ancil let her eyes roll. Did he think she was a baby? She wasn't likely to drop them. He showed her how to adjust the lenses to her own eyes, then directed her attention to some gulls tracking the beach nearby.

"See the dark mark at the tip of the bill?" he asked. "Those are ring-billed gulls. The larger ones are herring gulls."

She didn't really want his bird-watching lesson but knew she had to act cooperative in order to keep the binoculars. Eyepieces to her eyes, she focused on the gulls. She was surprised at the clarity with which she could see them— the size and color of the beak, the yellow eyes, the sleek smoothness of the feathers. Just as she was wondering what kind of gulls the dark ones were, but wouldn't ask, Harvey told her.

"The dark, mottled gulls are first-year herrings," he said. "The not-quite-so-mottled ones are second year, and the sleek silver ones are third year or older, fully mature."

She nodded and, glasses still to her eyes, walked away toward the gulls. The beach lurched and she lowered the glasses.

"I don't recommend trying to walk while looking through binoculars," he said. "Unless you like being seasick."

She walked away from his casual hominess. She took twelve steps before she stopped again and raised the glasses to her eyes. If she had known there was such a magic in the magnification, perhaps she would have asked for binoculars for a wedding present. She thought of the parrot she had so desired and how it hung shrouded in the corner of her room. If Harvey had given her binoculars, she'd hate them as she now hated the parrot. Poor parrot. Her feelings weren't reasonable. She admitted that. But as Mother said, feelings were neither right nor wrong. Feelings just were.

But Mother also said that if you wanted to, you could usually do something about your feelings. Perhaps when she got home she would unwrap the parrot.

She lifted the binoculars to her eyes again and watched the sandpipers. They walked with the quick, stiff-legged walk of people in a speeded-up old movie. Their footprints etched a design along the edge of the water. Was this what it was like to look through the telescope? she wondered. Pointing the glasses upward, she scanned the sky. Where was Venus? She had no idea where to look.

She swung down and around and focused on the family in the water. They were all there now. Gran, Mother, Margaret, and Lydia floated gracefully on the waves. Grandy swam parallel to the beach, and Harvey and Zan were playing toss-up. Ancil shivered. They were all such water people. Perhaps she had been born into the wrong family.

To take her attention away from them, she counted shrimp boats along the horizon until she was once more looking down the beach, walking, looking, walking, looking. When she noticed the family again, they were straggling out of the water and heading for the blankets.

The picnic was a feast. "An elaborate picnic is hard work," Mother had said, and anyone who was willing to prepare one could certainly do so. And today Harvey had. There were exclamations over the food as there had been over the totem pole. Fried chicken, potato salad, fresh broccoli with cheese sauce, and fruit salad of cantaloupe, watermelon, apples, peaches, and grapes. In addition, there was cheese and homemade bread and, for the adults, wine.

"Harvey, you've really outdone yourself," Grandy said, passing around the paper plates. Eating was accompanied by a chorus of appreciative mmm's.

After lunch they lolled on the blankets, resting, reading, talking. Feeling warm and tingly, Ancil realized she had forgotten the sunscreen. Uh-oh. She was already pink, and pink for her meant she'd already had too much sun.

"Let me help you," Harvey said when he saw her reach for the tube of lotion.

"Zan will do it," she said quickly, holding the tube toward Zan. Zan did not make a corresponding move, and Harvey's hand was reaching for the lotion. "Mo-therr," she said, in a wail for help, but Mother played deaf, too, and Harvey had his hand on the lotion. He squeezed some into his palm and began rubbing Ancil's back and shoulders. She gritted her teeth and closed her eyes. Such a difference in hands, she noticed. His was large and strong. He capped the lotion and set it down, and she lay face-down on the blanket, arms under her head, and pretended to go to sleep.

Voices hummed, talking of the weather and the sea. She

kept waiting for them to think she was asleep and begin talking about her, but they did not.

Margaret's voice stirred her. "There's your friend Lloyd."

Ancil sat up and followed Margaret's pointing finger. Sure enough Lloyd and a woman she assumed was his mother were crossing the beach toward the water. She stood up.

"Lloyd, Lloyd," she called.

"Hey, Ancil, spaghetti-head," he called in response when he'd seen her. "Come on in the water." He beckoned with a broad sweep of his arm. Ancil could see that, having persuaded his mother to bring him to the beach, he was not going to waste time socializing.

"I, uh, just ate," she called, glad of an excuse that sounded like a reason.

"It's been long enough," Mother said.

"Okay. Later," Lloyd called back. He walked into the water, stooping and throwing handfuls of water in the air. His mother stopped at the foam-flecked tideline and began to pace.

"She's afraid of the water," Ancil told her family. Lloyd waded into waist-deep water, right where the waves were breaking. "She's scared for him to be in the water." Lloyd plunged in and swam between breakers, standing up each time a breaker rolled onto him. One caught him and knocked him down. His mother's hand flew to her mouth, but Lloyd came up sputtering and grinning.

"Poor woman," Mother said. "She's scared to death."

They watched with a mixture of amusement and sympathy. At least, Ancil thought, she was not afraid for anyone else to go in the water, just herself.

"Come on, gang," Harvey said. "Let's go play near the boy, and he won't even knew he's being watched." He and the other girls hopped up.

"We're going to walk a bit," Gran said. She and Grandy hooked elbows and stepped off down the beach.

"I think I'll stay here and read," Mother said.

"Me, too," Ancil said, curling her arms around her shins. She meant stay here, not read, although she wished she had thought to bring a book. She'd have to remember next time. Lying on the beach blanket, reading, was an acceptable reason to stay out of the water. She saw Harvey go over and say something to Lloyd's mother before he splashed into the surf. "I guess he told her he'd watch out for Lloyd," Ancil said.

"Yes, I guess so," Mother said. She held a slim paperback book aloft and began to read.

Ancil read the title aloud. "*Steppenwolf*. What does that mean?"

"A wolf from the steppes," Mother said without looking up.

"Oh, a wolf story!" One of her favorite books was about a girl in Alaska who was lost in the wilderness but survived because of what her father had taught her about wolves. And she knew from geography that the steppes were like plains.

"Well, no, it's not exactly a wolf story," Mother said. "It's about a man who feels he is half man, half wolf."

"Ooooh, a werewolf," Ancil said, shuddering. She was not really a scary person, but she didn't like scary stories.

"Well, no." Mother lowered the book. "He doesn't turn into a wolf with whiskers and pointed teeth. It's internal. He feels partly tame and partly wild. It's about the opposite feelings we have sometimes."

Ancil nodded with understanding. "Like liking the water and not liking the water?"

"Uh-huh," Mother said. "Or loving your family and hating your family." Mother reached out and briefly touched Ancil's hand.

Arms still around her legs, Ancil rocked back and forth and stared at the shimmering, surging water. Even though she never went beyond the breakers without Mother, she hadn't been afraid of the water until the day Harvey had tossed her. There he was, tossing Zan now. Zan loved it. But everybody doesn't like everything, she assured herself. And it was Harvey who had made her afraid of the water. Or had she made herself afraid because she didn't like Harvey?

Her thoughts were so mixed up. Feelings were creeping in that almost made Harvey seem likable. To distract herself, she gathered a couple of paper cups and moved away from the blankets toward the water and began idly scraping sand.

Now Lloyd was starting to play with Harvey and Zan. Lyddy came out of the water and returned with the Frisbee. Ancil stared at the grains of sand, pretending not to notice the camaraderie taking place in the water. Harvey was like a blob of mercury, rolling around and gathering everyone into himself. What was the word they'd learned in science? Amalgamation? Well, she would not amalgamate. She was cast iron. She was not taken in by mercury.

There was a heap of sand now, and her scraping had left a moat around it. She began patting it, squaring up the sides, flattening the top, adding turrets by using the paper cups as molds. Suddenly a deep male voice called, "Heads up, Ancil." The Frisbee whizzed by her ear and sliced through a turret. It was Harvey, trying to draw her into the game. "Oops," he said when he saw what the Frisbee had done. She picked up the yellow saucer disk and flung it toward the sea. Didn't he ever give up? The Frisbee bit into the air, caught an updraft, and sailed directly over Harvey's head. He leaped, streaming water as he rose above it, stretched his arms and body upward, and caught the Frisbee.

"Good throw, Ancil," he called, and zipped it back to her before he fell back into the water. "Come on, play with us," he said, righting himself, brushing wet hair back from his forehead. "Be our landsider."

She picked up the Frisbee, tossed it into the sea, and turned her back before she saw who did or didn't catch it. She concentrated on her sand castle, filling in the moat, enlarging the castle, digging another moat, building a bridge across it.

"Wow, that's some fine castle," a voice said. Lloyd was there beside her. "I built one once."

"Only once?" She'd built dozens and dozens.

"This is just the third time in my life I've ever been to the beach. My last stepfather brought me the other two times."

His last. She remembered he'd said that he'd had two stepfathers.

"That's when I got the olive shell," he said.

She wondered if he was sorry he'd given it to her. She thought of offering to give it back but that might make Lloyd think she didn't treasure it. She looked at him, and he seemed to be lost in dreaming. "What are you thinking about?" she asked.

"I should have liked him more," Lloyd said. "He was a nice stepfather." His words were almost lost in the hiss of the sea. More clearly he said, "Can I help you?"

Now she was lost in thought. Was Harvey a nice stepfather? Zan thought so. Lydia thought so. Margaret, Mother, Gran, Grandy, everyone thought so. Everyone but her.

Lloyd mistook her silence for reluctance. "I'll do just what you say to do," he said. "You're the architect. I'll just follow your instructions. You want a turret, I'll build a turret. You want a dungeon, I'll build a dungeon."

She smiled. He couldn't have pleased her more. He didn't even know that her grandfather was an architect. Or that her father would have been. Or—the idea just occurred to her—that she might be an architect someday. Glass houses, not sand castles.

"Okay. A dungeon," she said. "I don't have a dungeon. Dig carefully and don't let the castle cave in."

With one finger he began digging at the backside of the castle. "You know what I do sometimes?" he said. "I build castles in my mind and put the people I don't like in the dungeon."

"Who will be in this dungeon?" she asked.

"Bobby," he said as he kept digging.

"Marcia," she said, and she added another turret.

"Shafer," he said.

Harvey, she thought, but didn't say it.

As if her thought had summoned him, there was Harvey beside her, looking taller than ever from where she sat, her head at his knee. Her sisters were there, too, all admiring the castle and clamoring to help. It had been a clamoring and exclaiming day, she thought—the totems, the picnic, and now her sand castle.

"Only if you build it her way," Lloyd said. "She's the architect."

"Oh, please. Let me do turrets," Zan said. "Where do you want some more turrets?"

"And a garden. Do you have a garden yet? It should have flowers and hedgerows and huge strange sculptures, like Stonehenge," Margaret said.

Imagine Margaret being interested in anything but looking for boys, Ancil thought. She gave directions for the locations of turrets and gardens.

"And you?" Ancil looked at Lydia. Lyddy nodded, indicating that she, too, wanted to help. "We need some outdoor space for the horses," Ancil said.

"Come on, Mother," Zan called, beckoning to Mother.

"Come on, Mama," Lloyd called to his mother, who was sitting alone a little distance away. "Mama can help, too, can't she?"

"Sure," Ancil said.

"May I make one turret?" Harvey asked. He was addressing both Ancil, as architect, and Zan, as chief turret builder. Zan handed him the cup and he added one turret, hollowing out the top and edging it expertly.

The castle was six feet around and still growing. Beachwalkers stopped by to watch and admire. Ancil directed Lloyd, Zan, Lydia, Margaret, Mother, Lloyd's mother. Harvey stepped away and came back with his camera, leaning, stooping, walking around and taking pictures from every angle.

Gran and Grandy appeared from down the beach.

"Harvey, get in the picture," Grandy said, reaching out to take the camera from Harvey. Harvey sat down beside Ancil and casually rested a hand on her shoulder. She closed her eyes, but he didn't seem to notice. Everyone was chattering, bragging about the castle, telling Gran and Grandy just what things they'd built.

"Could we put a picture in the paper, do you think?" Zan asked.

"We'll have to ask Ancil," Harvey said. His fingers pressed into her shoulder. As she hunched against it, she realized it didn't feel so bad, his hand, draping there. His hand on her shoulder was like a father's hand. She looked up at him in surprise, but he was not looking at her. He was looking and grinning into the camera. Perhaps, she thought, it would be a fine thing to have a picture of her sand castle in the paper, the *Hanover Historian*, reporting history as it happens. Harvey's *Hanover Historian*. When Grandy snapped the camera, Ancil was beginning to smile.